"THERE'S SOMETHING I HAVE TO KNOW," Marc murmured, closing the distance between them and sliding one hand under her loose hair to the nape of her neck.

In the seconds granted to her, Josie knew she could stop this. She *knew* she could. All she had to do was stiffen, or pull away, or just say no. *No, don't do that. No, I don't want to.*

Except that she did want to.

She gazed into his heavy-lidded, tarnished-silver eyes until his lips touched hers, and then she closed her own eyes as an abrupt wave of dizzy pleasure washed over her. His mouth was warm, soft and hard at the same time, and incredibly erotic. She could feel the tension of wariness seeping out of her, feel her body soften and begin to tremble.

She felt the tip of his tongue probing, sliding along the sensitive inner surface of her lip, and a hot shiver rippled through her. She had never felt anything like it before, and was astonished to realize it was desire. . . .

WHAT ARE *LOVESWEPT* ROMANCES?

They are stories of true romance and touching emotion. We believe those two very important ingredients are constants in our highly sensual and very believable stories in the LOVE-SWEPT line. Our goal is to give you, the reader, stories of consistently high quality that may sometimes make you laugh, sometimes make you cry, but are always fresh and creative and contain many delightful surprises within their pages.

Most romance fans read an enormous number of books. Those they truly love, they keep. Others may be traded with friends and soon forgotten. We hope that each LOVESWEPT romance will be a treasure—a "keeper." We will always try to publish

LOVE STORIES YOU'LL NEVER FORGET
BY AUTHORS YOU'LL ALWAYS REMEMBER

The Editors

Loveswept ® 703

THE HAUNTING OF JOSIE

KAY HOOPER

BANTAM BOOKS
NEW YORK · TORONTO · LONDON · SYDNEY · AUCKLAND

THE HAUNTING OF JOSIE

A Bantam Book / August 1994

*If you would be interested in receiving protective vinyl covers for
your Loveswept books, please write to this address for information:*

Loveswept
Bantam Books
P.O. Box 985
Hicksville, NY 11802

ISBN 0-553-44345-3

Published simultaneously in the United States and Canada

PROLOGUE

From his position at the top of a small rise, he could see the house clearly. It was a nice house. An interesting house, with the definite possibility of lots of nooks and crannies. The roof was angular with peaks and gables, and the numerous windows gleamed redly from the light of the setting sun. A wide porch, complete with aging wicker furniture, ran along two sides of the house and enticed with a view of the surrounding countryside.

In the fall the view was rather cheerless. The vibrant, colorful leaves of the hardwood trees had dropped long before, leaving their branches bare, and the grass of the hills looked bleached and curiously flattened. He could see a sprawling, overgrown garden in back of the house, the paths hardly more than rabbit trails winding among ragged hedges, ivy-covered benches, greenish birdbaths, browned and dried flowers, and naked rosebushes in desperate need of pruning.

Still, it was an oddly inviting place, placid in the momentary pause between hot weather and cold, solidly *there* as if its roots were planted deeply. Though the garden and surrounding land was obviously neglected, the house itself showed signs of recent repairs: new shingles covered the roof, a thick layer of pristine gravel coated the driveway, and the scent of fresh paint lingered in the still, cool air.

Just beyond the overgrown garden, he could see the roof of another structure, perhaps a small cottage that, in a richer age, might once have provided living quarters for a housekeeping couple or the gardener. Or it might have been designed for guests, an elegant—if inconvenient—attempt to provide privacy. He could see nothing else of the building, but since the shingles covering that roof also appeared new, it looked as if the cottage had seen the same recent repairs as the house.

He returned his gaze to the house, studying the rather battered van that was parked at the end of the sidewalk and was packed to the brim with boxes and bags. As he watched, a slender, red-headed young woman in jeans and a sweatshirt came out of the house and went to the van. He couldn't see what she was doing since the bulk of the vehicle blocked his view, but in just a few minutes she returned to the house heavily laden with several small boxes, one garment bag, and a closed umbrella.

Ah. Obviously, she was moving in.

When she disappeared through the front door, he made his way down the hill toward the house. The gravel of the driveway crunched pleasantly under his feet, and he paused a moment to examine the small white pebbles. Then he continued on until he reached the remains of what had once been a picket fence surrounding the small front yard; there was only a single post now where a gate had once stood, and the post that had once held a mailbox now provided only a crooked platform where the box would have sat.

He jumped up on that and sat, waiting.

When she came back down the sidewalk, the woman paused and regarded him in surprise. She looked tousled but not at all tired. Her bright hair was caught in an untidy braid, with escaping wisps of red that framed her face, and there was a smudge of something sooty on her nose. Her unusual violet eyes were very bright and vivid with energy.

"Well, hello. Where did you come from?"

He liked her voice. It was quiet yet lilting, and vibrant with the same interest that filled her eyes. He replied to her politely, offering greetings.

Her smile widened, and she reached out to touch him, careful until he raised his chin and purred happily. Then she scratched him in just the right way, her slim fingers deft and knowledgeable as they moved beneath his chin and behind his ears.

"The realtor said the owner was living somewhere on the place in a cottage," she remarked to him, still gently scratching. "I suppose you live with him?"

He ventured a somewhat muffled response, his eyes half-closed and chin still raised in bliss.

"Well, you're not a stray, that's for sure. You've obviously been fed and brushed on a regular basis. And then, there's this." With a last scratch, she reached for the silver tag hanging from his decorative collar and read the single word silently. She raised her eyebrows as she met his limpid gaze. This time her voice held definite surprise. "Pendragon?"

He affirmed this cordially.

She laughed. "Forgive me, please, but that's an odd name for a cat—even a black one. Are you somebody's familiar?"

He expressed scorn for this.

She laughed again, obviously understanding— his tone if not the actual language. "All right, I was just asking. Well, Pendragon, my name is Josie. It's nice to meet you."

Since she accompanied the words with a luxurious stroke all the way down his back, his throaty response was more than usually delighted.

"You're welcome to check the house for mice or bugs," she told him agreeably. "And you can even sleep on my bed as long as whoever else you own doesn't mind."

He appreciated the delicacy of her invitation; only cat people understood that cats were never *owned*; if there was any belonging, it was on the part of their humans. He accepted her offer with dignified pleasure.

She chuckled and scratched him briefly under his chin. "Okay. The front door's open, so you can explore inside, but I'd appreciate it if you stay out of my way while I'm carrying stuff in. The last thing I need is to break something falling over you. Got it?"

He indicated that he got it.

"Good. Then welcome to Westbrook. That's the name of the house, they tell me. It's named after the writer who built it back in the thirties."

She stepped to the van and began pulling more boxes out, still talking casually to the watching cat.

"I didn't know about the writer until after I signed the lease, but it seems a good omen to me. I mean, Luke Westbrook is supposed to have said this place inspired him to write, so maybe it'll help me with my work. Think it might, cat?"

Pendragon replied with a suitably ambiguous opinion, and watched as she gathered up two file boxes, a small suitcase, and another umbrella, to carry inside. When she staggered up the sidewalk toward the house, a hint of movement from another direction caught his attention, and he raised his gaze to one of the high windows to search out the source of the motion.

It was hardly more than a flicker, as though a curtain had been twitched back into place.

Pendragon watched for a moment longer, but

there was no further movement. He murmured something in the back of his throat and jumped off the mailbox platform. Tail held high, he strolled up the sidewalk toward the house.

Where there were lots of nooks and crannies.

ONE

"Excuse me, but—"

Josie nearly jumped out of her skin. Not only was the deep masculine voice unfamiliar, it was totally unexpected. Though there were houses scattered about the countryside, none was close enough to invite curious neighbors to stroll over, particularly on a dreary fall afternoon.

But even as she turned quickly away from her van to face him, she remembered that the owner of Westbrook was also staying "on the place" in a cottage, as the realtor had offhandedly explained. He hadn't explained a few other vital bits of information, however, and she was suddenly very conscious of her faded jeans, sloppy sweatshirt, and the disastrous state of her once-neat braid.

"I'm sorry, I didn't mean to startle you."

Josie looked up into apologetic gray eyes, and for an instant couldn't say a word. He had a slight southern accent, which she liked, and the words were certainly sincere enough—but neither was responsible for her silence. She wasn't a woman who judged someone on first appearances and, in fact, tended to be so cautious that she made up her mind only after knowing someone for quite a while—but her initial impression of this man was so positive it was bewildering.

It had to be his looks, she thought dazedly. Now she knew what "drop-dead gorgeous" *really* meant. He was a couple of inches over six feet with the wide-shouldered, powerful build of a natural athlete, ruggedly set off at the moment by jeans and a mostly blue flannel shirt. No wedding ring, which might or might not mean he was single. He had black hair—not dark, not sable, and not any shade of brown, but raven black—cut in a layered, neat style of medium length with short sideburns and a natural widow's peak as rare as it was dramatic.

His eyes were such a light gray they appeared almost silver, very sharp and vibrant, and they were set beneath winged brows as dramatic and memorable as the widow's peak. The rest of his face was just as striking, gifted with high cheekbones, a perfect nose, and a mouth that was utterly masculine and filled with sensuality and humor. He had a strong jaw that showed a great deal of character and perhaps just a touch of stubbornness.

All in all, it was a remarkable face.

Josie knew she stared up at him for only a few seconds, but it seemed much longer. Clearing her throat, she managed to say, "It's all right—I'd just forgotten you were staying at the cottage. That is, if you're the owner?"

He nodded and smiled. "Marc Westbrook."

"Westbrook?"

"An ancestor built the house back in the thirties," he explained. "It's been in the family, one way or another, ever since."

"I see." Gathering her scattered wits, she noticed two things then. One, that he was carrying Pendragon, and two, that his left arm—the one he was using to cradle the cat—was in a cast from elbow to knuckles. And since she had missed both those rather obvious facts while she'd stared at him like an idiot, it said a great deal about the effect he had on her.

For heaven's sake, she had noted the lack of a wedding band while completely missing the cast *and* the cat!

Belatedly recalling her manners, she extended a hand. "I'm Josie Douglas." She no longer expected people to react to the name; Douglas was fairly common, after all, and without the singularity of her father's name to stir memories, few knew who she was.

"Welcome to Westbrook, Josie Douglas," he replied.

His grip was firm but careful, the touch of a powerful man wary of his own physical strength. It was probably usual for him to be cautious because big men often were, she thought, but she also knew that she *did* look a bit fragile.

She had long considered it her curse that she frequently roused protective instincts in the men she met; she assumed it was because she was slender, small-boned, and always pale. She looked helpless, apparently. Never mind that she seldom needed help and even more rarely wanted it; few males asked, they simply tried to help her.

The handshake lasted just a bit longer than necessary, and Josie could have sworn her flesh actually tingled when the contact with his was broken. *Ridiculous. Of course it's ridiculous.* What on earth was wrong with her?

Conjuring up what she hoped was an impersonal smile, she said, "I met Pendragon a couple of hours ago."

"Met him? I thought he was yours," Marc Westbrook said, with a glance down at the cat in his arms. "That's why I came over here, to return him to you."

She looked into the enigmatic china-blue eyes of the big black cat, then shook her head. "No, he just showed up a couple of hours ago. But he can't be a stray, surely?"

"I wouldn't think so, he's been too well fed— and he certainly doesn't have the beat-up, ragged appearance of a stray tomcat. But I've been out here for nearly two months, and the first I saw of him was when he rattled my screen door a few minutes ago." He set the cat on the mailbox platform, and Pendragon curled his tail around his forepaws and regarded them both placidly.

His eyes were definitely odd for a black cat, Josie reflected. They were Siamese eyes, vibrant blue and just faintly crossed, yet he didn't show any other sign of Oriental ancestry. He was large-boned and solid rather than slender, and his glossy black coat didn't have so much as a speck of white anywhere that she could see. And he was unusually large, weighing every ounce of what Josie guessed to be twenty pounds.

"Do you suppose he belongs to one of the neighbors, then?" Josie suggested, but rather doubtfully.

"As I'm sure you noticed on the drive out, neighbors are few and far between. Most of the land around these parts is pastured. There's a horse farm about two miles or so from here—they raise Thoroughbreds—and maybe half a dozen houses within a ten-mile radius, but that's it."

Josie knew; one of the reasons she'd picked this place was its virtual isolation. Of course, that was when she'd imagined the owner of Westbrook as being some elderly man, a widower, perhaps, who was renting out the main house because it had gotten too big for him, or something like that. But she should have asked. She really should have asked. Because she certainly hadn't expected a devastatingly handsome man somewhere in his mid-thirties with vivid eyes and a lazy voice who liked cats and seemed to have time on his hands. . . .

What a landlord.

"He might belong to somebody around here," Marc Westbrook was going on, "but I wouldn't know who to ask."

Concentrating on the conversation, she said, "Then I guess we should give him the run of the place and see if he sticks around. If he does . . . an ad in the local paper asking if anyone's missing a black cat?"

"Suits me. We'll give it a few days. As a matter of fact, it's nice to have a cat around."

"They're good company," she agreed. "And Pendragon seems very polite."

Marc smiled. "Agreed. So, we'll wait and see. And we'll let him decide whose bed he takes over at night."

There was a brief silence that Josie found a bit unnerving. Casting about, she gestured slightly toward his left arm and asked, "An accident?"

"So they said. A drunk driver crossed over the median and I couldn't get out of his way."

"I'm sorry."

"So was he." Marc didn't seem to think that needed elaboration, because he continued in a lighter tone. "As far as I was concerned, it wasn't all bad. I hadn't had a vacation in years, and I hadn't realized how badly I needed one until I spent most of the first couple of weeks sleeping. The injuries were relatively simple; the ribs knit, and the cast came off my leg two weeks ago, so all I have to put up with is the inconvenience of having a cast on my left arm."

"You're left-handed?"

"Wouldn't you know it? Murphy's law. But even it's better now than it was; the damn thing started out covering the entire arm."

The explanation answered Josie's major question, but she asked anyway. "So you're convalescing?"

"That's the idea. My doctor thought I wouldn't rest in the city—I work in Richmond—so knowing I owned this property, he insisted I exile myself out here. Unfortunately for me, my doctor also happens to be my best friend from college, so he considers it his right to push me around."

Josie had the shrewd notion that nobody pushed Marc Westbrook around, not even his best friend, but she didn't say so. Instead she said, "I'd say this would be a good place to heal. Quiet. Peaceful."

His mouth twisted slightly, and the silvery eyes gleamed with amusement. "Yeah, right. Miles away from everything, and too far out for cable; so far, I've resisted the lure of a satellite dish, but it's only a matter of time until I give in to my lesser self. For the first time since college, I'm caught up on my reading, and I've discovered a dozen new ways to play solitaire."

"Bored?"

"Well, let's put it this way—the arrival of the

mailman is the high point of my day; I have all the Richmond newspapers sent out here, as well as several from surrounding cities." His smile became even more crooked. "Until the accident, I led the very busy, not to say frantic, lifestyle of a criminal lawyer, and all this peace and quiet is driving me nuts."

She was amused and not unsympathetic, but also a bit uneasy. While there was nothing wrong with having an attractive man nearby—she was a normal woman, after all—she had an awful lot to do and only a year in which to do it, and she certainly didn't want anyone looking over her shoulder while she did it. Particularly not a criminal lawyer. Of course, since Marc was obviously recovered except for the arm, he would no doubt be returning to Richmond and work soon.

Probing as delicately as possible, she asked, "It won't be much longer, surely? I mean, after two months?"

"If my friend the doctor has his way, a few more weeks. This cast is due to come off in thirteen days—precisely—and after that it shouldn't be more than a couple of weeks before he has to admit I'm fit for work."

Josie couldn't help smiling, but her amusement changed to embarrassment when he went on dryly.

"So you don't have to be afraid I'll make a nuisance of myself for too long."

"I didn't—"

He chuckled, a low sound of genuine amusement. "No, you didn't say so, but I don't blame you for wondering. I'll admit, finding out I'd have a tenant in the house raised my spirits a bit, and I do hope you won't get too upset with me if I borrow a cup of sugar now and then—but I promise I won't try to use you to alleviate my boredom."

"Fair enough." She managed to keep her voice light, but she knew her face was still filled with color because she could feel the heat. It was another of her curses; her skin was very pale, but embarrassment instantly brought a vibrant blush to her cheeks. It gave her away every time, dammit. But at least he didn't comment.

"Good. Now—that said, can I help you unload the van?"

Josie had brought the first load of her belongings to the house early this morning; this was the second and final load, and it was a bit sobering that all her worldly possessions—except for quite a few boxes of books that were in storage—could be stuffed in the cramped space of two vans. . . . She glanced behind her at the vehicle, still about a quarter full, then at her watch. It was almost five, and with winter approaching, it would soon be dark.

She hesitated for an instant, then said, "I think I'll leave the rest until tomorrow."

Mildly, he said, "I can manage pretty well even with the cast, you know."

Josie eyed him. "I don't doubt it. But I've had

enough for one day, I think. Look, I was going to make some coffee—would you like some?"

"I'd love some," he accepted promptly. "Even with a coffee maker, I don't seem to have the knack."

"How do you know I do?" she asked in a wry tone as she reached back to close the van's side door.

"I don't—but the odds say your coffee has to be better than mine."

"We'll see." But she wasn't too worried, because the truth was she knew she could make very good coffee. She used a specially blended fresh-ground variety filled with taste. And a percolator.

As if he had understood their conversation, Pendragon jumped down from his perch and preceded them up the sidewalk to the house, his tail high. Dignified.

Josie had a hunch that the cat would indeed stick around, for a while, and that a newspaper ad would produce no one who had misplaced a beloved pet. There was just something *about* Pendragon, an air of independence and pride even greater than usual for a feline, and it spoke of self-sufficiency. Still, someone had certainly fastened the decorative collar around his neck and provided a name tag. . . .

He had been somebody's cat long enough to earn himself a peculiar name, at least.

She dismissed thoughts of the cat as they went into the house, leading the way through the jumble of boxes and furniture still under dustcovers while Marc followed her.

"I should have had this place cleaned before you moved in," he said suddenly. "The last time must have been right after the interior was painted, and that was six months ago. I'd forgotten how dusty a house could get."

She glanced back over her shoulder to see him frowning slightly as he looked around. "A little dust certainly isn't going to hurt me," she told him. "Besides, I'm sure I'll settle in better if I spend the first few days cleaning for myself. It's an excellent way to get to know a house."

"I could get somebody out here—"

"No, please, I'd rather do it myself." She pushed open the swinging door leading to the kitchen.

Following, Marc said, "If you're sure." He looked around at the bright kitchen, which boasted a line of windows along one side to admit plenty of light, and was painted a cheerful pale yellow. The remodeling work had gone well in here, he decided, and the decision to practically rebuild the room had definitely been the right one.

All the appliances were new, as well as the deep double sink and sparkling fixtures; the tile countertops had been redone in a lovely white marbleized pattern, and the original old wooden table in the center of the spacious room had been replaced by a combination breakfast bar and work island. But even with all the improvements, the room still retained the cheeriness and warmth Marc remembered from his childhood.

"Have a seat," Josie invited, gesturing toward one of the stools at the breakfast bar. She went to the counter beside the sink, where her percolator was already set out with the bag of coffee. There were several boxes on the counter containing her kitchen things, and a number of dry goods stacked here and there ready to be put away in the pantry; she had already unpacked perishable groceries earlier and placed the food in the refrigerator.

"I meant to tell you before," she commented. "This is a great house."

"Thanks, I think so. Plenty of character. It was in pretty good shape when I bought it a few years ago," he offered, taking a stool at the bar. "Structurally, anyway. It was built back when houses were intended to stand for a hundred years."

Josie filled the percolator and set it up, looking over at him curiously. "You said this place had belonged to your family since it was built?"

"Yes—though it hasn't been lived in for any length of time since Luke Westbrook's death."

"Why not?"

"I don't think anybody had the nerve at first; the house was probably closed up for a good ten years or so after his younger brother—my grandfather—inherited it. Since then, it's been mostly used as a summer house, and passed fairly rapidly from hand to hand until I bought it from an uncle."

Josie turned and leaned back against the counter, frowning slightly. "Wait a minute. You don't think anybody had the nerve to live here? Have I missed something?"

"Mmm. The realtor told me there were things tenants had no need to know, but . . ." He eyed her, a slight smile playing about his mouth. "Do you spook easily?"

"Not so far." She smiled in spite of herself. "Out with it. I've leased a haunted house?"

Marc shook his head. "Nothing so colorful, I'm afraid. I stayed here during quite a few summers while I was a kid, and I can tell you there was never so much as a creaking floorboard or the rattle of a ghostly chain to disturb the night—to the intense disappointment of my cousins and myself. No, it's human tragedy rather than the supernatural, but quite a few people are either spooked by it —or squeamish. Luke Westbrook committed suicide here in 1944."

She winced. "How?"

"Shot himself. In that front parlor. At the time it was his study."

Great. Just where I plan to work. But she didn't say it aloud. Instead she said, "I knew who he was, of course; I love mysteries, and I've read most of his books. But I had no idea he'd killed himself."

"It was a hell of a story in those days, and got worldwide coverage even with the war going on," Marc said musingly. "He was fairly young—in his late thirties—and a very successful mystery writer."

"Then why did he kill himself?"

"According to the note he left, he was convinced he couldn't write anymore—it had been more than a year since his last book was published —and didn't want to live the rest of his life trading on existing work and trying to recapture past glory. Or words to that effect. He seemed to feel his only worth was as a writer, and if he couldn't do that, and do it as well as he had for the better part of ten years, he didn't want to go on. Apparently, he was well known for having a mercurial temperament, so nobody was much surprised."

"So the death of a famous mystery writer wasn't a mystery?"

"Ironic, huh? Judging by some of the remarks I heard from older relatives when I was a kid, I gather the family rather thought old Luke had let them down in more ways than one. A juicy murder would have been preferable to a tawdry suicide."

"People being what they are," Josie agreed ruefully.

"Yeah." He studied her for a moment, the pale gray eyes intent. "So you aren't bothered by the shadow of violence under this roof?"

"That's a nice way to put it. No, I'm not bothered. I imagine most old houses have seen episodes of violence. In fact, I once lived in a house where two separate murders had taken place years before. But since there were no mysterious stains on the carpet or ghostly footsteps on the stairs in the wee small hours of the night, I wasn't disturbed."

He smiled. "In case you're wondering, that front room has been completely redone a number of times during the last fifty years. Even the fireplace has been sandblasted."

"I wasn't feeling squeamish," she assured him.

"Good. Now . . . since you've heard all about this house and me, what about you? What compels you to spend a winter way out here in the back of beyond—alone?"

Josie stepped aside to rummage in one of the boxes for a couple of coffee cups and spoons, hoping the action looked more casual than it was. With only a brief hesitation she replied in a light, slightly dry tone. "If you must know, I decided to take a year off my job—I'm a teacher—and find out if I really have the guts and the ability to write." Which was certainly true, as far as it went.

"You don't look old enough to be a teacher."

Josie knew he was fishing. She also knew that she looked a good ten years younger than she was. Resigned, she said, "I'm twenty-eight."

"You still don't look old enough to be a teacher." He was smiling.

"The eight-year-olds I teach haven't noticed." She put cups and spoons on the bar, then rummaged in another box for the canister of sugar she remembered packing.

"None of my teachers ever looked like you. Even when I was eight."

It was the sort of comment, Josie thought, that was usual between a man and woman, expressing tentative interest and inviting a response. She was too much a woman not to feel pleased, but too wary to respond with encouragement. This was hardly the best time in her life to get involved with anyone, given what she had come here to do. And, besides, a mending lawyer on the verge of ending his country exile was doubtless not the best man with whom to get involved.

So, ignoring what he'd said, she merely said, "Ah, the sugar. I knew it was here somewhere. Do you take cream—milk?"

"Milk if you have it."

"I have it. I think." She got a slender carton from the refrigerator and placed it and the sugar on the bar. Behind her, the percolator was bubbling, and the rich aroma of coffee filled the room.

He sniffed appreciatively, but what he said had nothing to do with coffee. "Do you wear contacts?"

"No. And my hair is really this color. I swear." Her voice was resigned once again. He was hardly the first to ask that question, and she understood all it implied; nobody ever believed that someone with hair as red as hers could also have pale violet eyes.

Marc chuckled suddenly. "Sorry. I seem to be asking all the obvious questions."

Reminding herself that a lawyer was trained to hear nuances in people's voices and adept at reading them correctly, Josie managed to smile at him. "Well, a few of them. I know I look like a kid, and the coloring is a bit weird. And, before you ask, I'm a lot stronger than I look—and not at all sickly."

"I'll try to remember that." He didn't say anything else until the coffee was poured. After taking a sip, he sighed and murmured, "If there's a secret, I wish you'd share it."

Josie nearly gasped in surprise before she realized that he was talking about the coffee. Of course he was talking about the coffee. But if she started jumping whenever he said things like that, she was going to arouse his courtroom instincts for sure, she knew that.

"No secret. I guess some people are just born with the knack," she managed.

"You're definitely one of them."

"Thanks."

There was a short silence that Josie was too unnerved to break. It was left to Marc, who asked what he probably assumed was an innocuous question.

"So this is a kind of sabbatical for you?"

"You could say that, I guess. I worked hard during the past few years to save enough so I could take a year off and get out of the city to try writing. I taught during the day, and did research and typed term papers for college students at night. I lived in Washington."

He nodded slightly, his gaze never leaving her face. "Did you pick this place because of Luke Westbrook?"

She shook her head. "No, the realtor told me about him only after I'd signed the lease. I didn't go looking for the former home of a writer. I wanted a place out in the country, peace and quiet. As soon as I saw the photos, I knew this house would suit me."

"Am I being too nosy?" he asked her, having obviously noted her dry voice.

"It's probably a character flaw of lawyers," she replied, still dry.

"I should probably try to defend myself on that point—but all I'll say is that it's nice to have somebody to talk to, and you'll have to forgive me if I get carried away."

Josie wondered how a grown man could sound so damned wistful, and even as she warned herself that lawyers were also innate actors, she could feel herself weakening. With a sigh, she said, "I don't really mind—but don't you think we've both asked enough questions for the first hour?"

"Is that a polite request for me to leave?"

"Of course not. You haven't finished your coffee."

Chuckling, he did so. "All right, Josie Douglas, I'll get out of your way and let you get settled in. But you have to let me repay you for the coffee. I happen to make the best spaghetti sauce in the state, and it's no fun at all to cook for just one. Tomorrow night at the cottage?"

Josie's hesitation was momentary. "If I can bring the bread and salad, you're on."

"Great. Is seven all right?"

"I'll be there."

She saw him out the back door, and as he went down the steps and walked away from her, she noted that he was favoring his right leg, though it was more of a tentativeness than a limp. Obviously, it was a lingering effect from the broken leg. With the cast off two weeks, he was probably regaining strength and mobility slowly but steadily.

Josie watched from the back door as he wound his way through the overgrown garden toward the cottage she could barely make out beyond tall and unruly hedges, and wondered if she was crazy. Her interest in Marc Westbrook was perfectly understandable, of course, but it was out of character for her to let down her guard—even a little bit—so quickly.

Out of character . . . and dangerous. She couldn't afford to trust anybody, not until she'd done what she had to do, what she'd planned for so many long years. It could all fall apart if the wrong person found out. Even now—especially now—she had to be careful.

Her purse was on the counter not far from the percolator. She went to it and slid a hand inside, then drew out a dark and deadly little automatic. She held the gun in her hand, the weight familiar and reassuring. She wouldn't need it, she told herself firmly. Not out here.

But she kept the gun within reach, nonetheless.

TWO

The furnace died with a gasp and a thud around one in the morning, and she was too tired and sleepy to get out of bed and try to figure out what was wrong with it. Hardly an emergency situation, she assured herself drowsily. A few hours without heat wasn't going to kill her. Surely she'd be all right until morning. . . .

Unfortunately for Josie, the night was a cold one, and a brisk wind searched out and explored all the chinks in the old house's armor with sadistic glee. She could feel several drafts blowing through her bedroom every time she poked her head out from under the scanty covers.

Bedding hadn't been included as part of her lease, so she'd brought her own, but most of that was still packed in one of the boxes downstairs; Josie had made her bed with sheets and only one thin blanket, too weary to take the time to hunt for the thick quilt and several other blankets she'd brought along.

Shivering, she invited the visiting black cat, who had remained companionably in the house all evening and accompanied her to bed, to get under the meager covers with her. She was pleased when he accepted. Some cats didn't like to sleep under covers or other things, but this one promptly curled up at her side, his unusually large and warm body radiating enough heat to counter some of the chill.

Even so, it was hardly the most comfortable night she'd spent, and when Pendragon woke her early the next morning by licking her nose and murmuring to her urgently, she felt the leaden weariness of someone whose body had been tensed against the cold for too many hours.

"It's like an icebox in here," she grumbled, pushing his face out of the way so she could draw the covers up over her head. The black cat was stubborn, burrowing his way back under the covers until he could find and lick her nose again.

Since even the gentlest cat was gifted by nature with a tongue like sandpaper, Josie knew her nose would soon be raw if she didn't give in to his determination. She pushed both him and the covers away and snatched the robe lying across the foot of her bed. Not that the thin garment helped; the room really *was* like an icebox.

She found her bedroom slippers, which were plush and offered real insulation against the chill of the wooden floors. It was only then that she noticed the face of her electric alarm clock was dark, and an experimental flick of the light switch confirmed her suspicions.

Great. Not just the furnace, but the power.

Accompanied by Pendragon, she went downstairs. His urgency was explained when he went immediately to the front door, and she let him out with a murmured apology. Cats, she knew, disliked having to ask the aid of their humans in their comings and goings; if Pendragon decided to stick around, she'd have to ask Marc about installing a pet door.

The house, dimly lit in the gray morning, looked a bit eerie as she passed through on her way to the kitchen. Boxes were stacked here and there, and dustcovers remained over most of the furniture downstairs. But, as she'd told Marc, Josie wasn't easily spooked, and she was too cold to care about anything except restoring power to the house.

A box of kitchen utensils yielded one of her flashlights, and the cellar door opened with a groan when she used a little muscle. She went down the wooden steps and into total blackness; the cellar had no windows to admit even dim light.

In the beam of her flashlight, she saw an incredible jumble of crates, boxes, and trunks crammed into the dark, earthy-smelling space. Shelves lined one wall and held dozens of sealed jars from the days when canning had been prevalent in "country" households, and another wall was covered with pegs holding items ranging from two shovels and a rake to bits of leather that looked to Josie like something from a horse's harness.

Shaking off fascination, she ignored the lure of old steamer trunks and stacked boxes, reminding herself that she was only a tenant here; the Westbrook family might have saved everything they'd ever owned, but that didn't mean she had any business pawing through their stuff. Her only legitimate business down here was to find—ah, there it was. The switch box.

The realty company had assured her that the house boasted a completely updated wiring system *and* a new furnace—a heat pump, actually—but Josie was familiar enough with old houses to check the obvious first. And sure enough, she discovered that something had kicked off the main breaker during the night. If it happened again, she told herself, she would definitely call an electrician out here to find out what was going on.

She cautiously reset the breaker and was instantly rewarded when a light near the foot of the steps came on. She also heard the hum of the refrigerator in the kitchen and was pretty sure of the distant thud of the heat pump coming on.

She picked her way back across the cellar, frowning a bit as she eyed the naked light bulb dangling from the ceiling near the foot of the steps. That was odd. She distinctly remembered opening the cellar door yesterday just long enough to glance into the black maw of steps; there had been no light on down here, and she hadn't turned one on.

She went back up the steps and the light went out obediently when she flipped the switch just inside the door.

"Gremlins," she murmured to herself. She shut the cellar door firmly, turned off her flashlight, and went about the normal morning business of fixing coffee and trying to wake up.

Pendragon made his reappearance a few minutes later, and she let him in the back when he rattled the screen door imperiously. He obviously expected breakfast, so she rummaged among boxes until she found a can of tuna, which he was pleased to devour delicately; a big cat, he had a big appetite.

Mindful that the hot-water heater needed time to get back up to speed, she elected to skip her usual morning shower. She carried her coffee back upstairs, braved the cold water to wash her face and brush her teeth, then dressed in jeans and a comfortable knit sweater.

By the time she returned to the ground floor, the coffee and warm clothing had made her much more comfortable. She wandered through a few of the downstairs rooms, musing about which ones she would use and ultimately deciding that the house was too nice to have any part of it closed up. She avoided the front parlor, not so much because of the tragic death that had occurred in the room but because all the file boxes containing twenty years of hard work were waiting there for her.

She wasn't ready to face that just yet.

It was barely eight o'clock when Josie went out onto the wide, inviting porch that ran along the front and one side of the house. She strolled toward the rear of the house, sipping her coffee and enjoying the crisp, chilled air of the morning. When she ran out of porch, she leaned against the sturdy railing and stood gazing over the garden. It must have been lovely once, she mused, with neat paths and the heavy and rich scent of flowers. It was a shame it had been let go.

She'd lived in apartments for most of her life, but Josie had always felt drawn to plants and flowers, and she'd frequently spent a few dollars of her weekly grocery money on houseplants. She had a green thumb, apparently; plants did well for her. She'd had to give all hers away when she left Washington, choosing not to try moving them.

Maybe, if Marc didn't mind, she'd work on the garden here this spring. After all, she couldn't spend every hour in the house, and the physical work out in the fresh air would certainly do her good. She could even do some work before spring, pruning and clearing away brush. . . .

Her gaze drifted across the garden as a movement caught her attention, and she saw a dark man in jeans and a sweatshirt moving away through the woods beyond the cottage. Marc. He seemed to be following a very faint path, Josie thought. Probably one he followed every morning. The doctor would have suggested walking to strengthen his leg after the cast came off, and the rolling hills around here would provide a good workout for the various muscles.

She watched him until he disappeared over a rise. She sipped her coffee, then held the cup away and stared at it thoughtfully. After a moment she went back into the house and to the kitchen. Pendragon was sitting on one of the barstools washing a forepaw, but looked up to greet her politely.

"You're a responsive cat, aren't you?" she commented, digging into the last remaining box in the kitchen to be unpacked.

"Yah," Pendragon replied, and bent his head to begin chewing on one of his claws.

"It's a bad sign to bite your nails," Josie told him severely. "Still, I'd rather you bit them than ruined Marc's furniture sharpening them."

"Ppprupt," the cat mumbled, still working on his manicure.

Josie decided she'd better stop talking to him until he finished; he could bite off something important while trying to answer her. Anyway, she finally found what she'd been looking for. She studied the thermos, checking it for cracks or other damage, then went to the sink to rinse it out. This was probably not a good idea, she told herself. For her to go to all this trouble demonstrated far too much interest in Marc. He could get the wrong idea about her intentions.

But she could stick a note on the thermos when she hung it from the cottage's doorknob to greet him when he came back home, explaining this as being no more than a neighborly gesture. After all, anyone would appreciate hot—and good —coffee waiting for them upon their return from a long walk on a chilly morning. She was just being a good neighbor.

That was all.

She had the last of her things out of the van by ten that morning, and it didn't take long to get everything put away. The morning had warmed enough so that she elected to turn off the heat and open a few windows; airing out the house for a few hours seemed like a good idea, since it had stood empty for so long, and all the activity had her warm enough.

By lunchtime, the dustcovers were off all the furniture, the kitchen was spotless, and the den was well on its way. Josie took a break to make herself a light meal, and that was when she discovered she had no bread—but all the fixings to make several loaves as well as a few batches of muffins. Though she couldn't remember buying the stuff, she wasn't surprised; she frequently made her own bread because it was one of the things her mother had taught her as a child.

Perked coffee *and* fresh-baked bread? The man would probably think she was aiming for his heart by way of his stomach. Great. She'd insisted on cleaning the house herself, and even if he didn't know it yet, she had designs on his garden. And she taught school to little kids.

Just your typical tough-minded career woman.

Josie sighed and began making bread. She had to eat, after all. Maybe he wouldn't notice that the bread she brought for their meal tonight was homemade. And if he did . . . well, it wouldn't matter. She felt far too wary of him to relax in his presence, so her prickly attitude would doubtless counteract whatever domestic points he might have tallied up in her favor.

She caught herself giggling as she kneaded dough. What on earth was wrong with her? Even if matrimony had been a goal of hers—which it definitely wasn't—Marc hadn't given so much as a dim sign that he was looking for a wife, domesticated or otherwise. In fact, common sense suggested that would be the last thing on his mind. All he wanted was something—anything—to relieve his boredom while he finished healing. A little harmless flirting was probably as far as he would go.

And that was fine with her. They could enjoy occasional wary companionship over a meal, fence verbally to amuse each other—and in a few weeks he'd return to Richmond.

Josie found that unaccountably depressing, and

the realization bothered her. After all, she was accustomed to being alone, and she'd always been content with her own company. She had learned, by necessity, to be independent and self-sufficient at a very young age. Her father had been too busy and preoccupied to be much of a companion at any time, and she'd been completely on her own for the ten years since his death. Before that, she had always taken care of him, especially during the last five years of his life after her mother had gone.

So the prospect of being alone again, even way out here, shouldn't have made her feel so low. Especially considering the fact that she had met Marc Westbrook only yesterday. He was too new to her life to be having *any* kind of effect on it.

"Yaaah?"

Wiping her hands on a dishtowel, Josie turned from the counter and her bread making to find Pendragon sitting pointedly by the cellar door. "I gather you want to go down there?"

"Yah."

"It looked awfully clean for a cellar; I bet you won't find any bugs or mice."

"Pprupp."

"You don't say." She caught herself smiling as she went to pull the door open for the cat. He stood there looking down at the stairs, then looked up at her and spoke sternly.

"Forgive me," she murmured, and leaned over to flip the switch on the wall. The light at the foot of the stairs came on, obedient to her touch.

The black cat murmured something in his throat and descended regally.

Chuckling, Josie left the cellar door open just a few inches and went back to her bread making. She liked cats very much, but she'd never shared her home with one. Even though many felines were apparently perfectly content with apartment life, Josie had elected not to have a pet because she spent so many hours away from home.

But she thought now that might have been a mistake. A pet might have helped her feel more . . . connected these last few years. Certainly less alone. She'd read somewhere that people with pets tended to be healthier as well as happier, and God knew there was something especially cheerless about coming home to an empty, silent apartment.

Deciding that she was depressing herself for no good reason, Josie turned on her portable radio and found some music she liked, and listened to that while she ate her lunch. She cleaned up afterward, checked on the progress of the bread, then took her radio into the den to finish cleaning in there.

It was about an hour later that she looked up from polishing a small table near a window and saw that Pendragon had emerged from the cellar. And he'd brought her a gift.

"All right, what is it?" she asked, approaching warily.

The big black cat made a soft, curiously contented sound and reached out a paw to bat at his offering. He looked up at her, obviously awaiting praise.

Josie's misgivings about dead or mortally wounded victims faded as she knelt before the cat. Lying on the polished wooden floor near glossy forepaws was a tarnished brass key. It looked old-fashioned and plain except for the loop of red satin ribbon, faded and threadbare, that might have been used to hang the key on a hook somewhere.

She held the key up and studied it. For a door somewhere in the house? She didn't think so. The doors here were big, paneled things with ornate knobs, and took keys much bigger than this one. She supposed it might have been designed for some kind of small box, perhaps a jewelry box belonging to one of the Westbrook ladies who had lived or stayed here during the past fifty years or so. The cat must have found it in the cellar—possibly still inserted into its lock—and was attracted by the dangling ribbon.

Gazing at Pendragon, she said, "I don't suppose you'd show me where you found this?"

He yawned.

"I didn't think so." Josie sighed.

"Homemade bread?"

Getting defensive about it, Josie decided, would only make matters worse. "Yes, my mother taught me how to make it when I was a kid," she told Marc casually.

"It smells great."

"So does your spaghetti sauce." She looked around the surprisingly spacious kitchen of the small cottage. It had that domain-of-a-cook appearance, with plenty of pots, pans, and utensils; a place for everything and everything in its place. He was clearly quite at home in it, and she thought ruefully that he was probably a much better cook than she was despite his inability to make coffee. He had thanked her solemnly for the morning gift of "wonderful" hot coffee the moment she'd arrived at the cottage.

Returning her gaze to Marc, who was stirring the sauce, she said, "Why do I get the feeling that you're probably a pretty good cook for a lawyer?"

He chuckled. "Something my father taught me. He believed in equality between the sexes, so there was no such thing as a 'traditional' role in our house. So I can cook, clean, and sew on buttons—and my sister's a first-rate mechanic. Of course, she can also cook and I can overhaul an engine. Dad was a very thorough man."

"And a handy one, from the sound of it." Josie was smiling. "So what does your sister do now?"

"She trains racehorses in Kentucky," Marc replied. "Anne has a veterinarian husband, three kids, and a houseful of pets of various kinds."

At the reference to pets, Josie automatically glanced toward the screen door leading from the kitchen to the back porch, but there was no sign of Pendragon. He had asked to be let out a few minutes before she had headed for the cottage, and she hadn't seen him anywhere in the garden.

Marc might have been following her thoughts because, without looking at her, he added, "Speaking of which—where's our feline visitor?"

"Outside somewhere." Josie hesitated, then said, "He wanted down in the cellar a few hours ago, and the next time I saw him he had a brass key with a faded ribbon attached to it. Do you have any idea what it might belong to?"

"Offhand, no, but feel free to look for yourself," Marc invited amiably. "I haven't been in the cellar in years, but I seem to remember that the family kept practically everything we ever owned —and most of it down there."

"I wouldn't feel right going through that stuff," she objected. "It belongs to you—"

"There's nothing personal down there, Josie, just the kind of junk families store in cellars and forget about. If you're curious about the key, you're welcome to explore; if you like cellars and attics—which some people do—you have my permission to rummage around all you want. Of course, if you do happen to stumble over a lost Rembrandt or something . . ."

"Of course," she agreed dryly.

He smiled at her, and Josie told herself that the leap in her pulse was merely because she loved exploring cellars and attics. *Yeah, right.*

The cottage was too small to have a separate dining room, but it did boast a breakfast nook with a bay window, and a small wooden table with two chairs gave the area a cozy appeal. They ate their meal there, and the food was so good that conversation was desultory until they finished. Afterward Josie helped him clear the table and load the dishwasher, and they ended up on the couch in the living room, where a cheerful fire burned in the fireplace.

"Why can't I make it taste this way?" he wondered ruefully, sipping the coffee that Josie had made using his coffee maker.

"We each have our little talents," she reminded him in a consoling tone of voice.

"I guess. But it isn't logical, you know. I watched you make this, and you did *exactly* what I do."

"Ah—but you didn't hear me murmur the magic spell."

Marc peered into his cup with a frown. "You didn't sprinkle a little eye of newt or toe of bat while I wasn't looking, did you?"

"Of course not. Today's magic spells are much more sophisticated. I used dragon's teeth."

"Which you just happened to find lying by the side of the road, I suppose?"

"Don't be ridiculous. Everyone knows dragons shed their teeth every leap year and pass them out only to redheaded witches with purple eyes and black cats."

After a moment's thought Marc said judiciously, "Your eyes are violet, not purple."

Josie had been enjoying the nonsense, but she felt her pulse give another of those peculiar little leaps when he looked at her with a faint smile and an intent gaze. His eyes were like very slightly tarnished silver, she thought, and with his dramatic black hair, widow's peak, and flying brows, he would have made an excellent warlock.

More nonsense.

Making her voice light, she said, "Well, you can't deny that my hair is red. Very red. And I do have a black cat, even if it's only temporarily."

"True." With a faint smile still playing about his mouth, he said, "You also have walls about a foot thick."

The observation startled her, and she knew he saw it. "We just met yesterday, in case you've forgotten."

Marc shook his head. "That isn't it, Josie. We've been fairly casual with each other, and talked all through dinner, but every time I asked a question about you—especially about your background—you were evasive and guarded."

Josie leaned forward to set her cup on the coffee table. She was trying to give herself time to think, but it was difficult when her awareness of him was so strong and when he was so close. There was no more than a foot of space between them, and that was too little for her peace of mind.

"You're imagining things," she managed finally. She leaned back, half turned toward him as before, and met his gaze, trying to keep her own calm and unexpressive.

"I don't think so."

She smiled. "I think you've been so bored that you're looking for any excuse to sharpen your lawyerly skills. But I'm not on the witness stand, counselor."

"I never thought you were."

"Funny. That's what it sounded like to me." Josie knew she sounded too defensive, but she couldn't help herself. She had spent too many years *feeling* defensive about who she was to be able to let go of that. Not now, at least. Not yet.

"I'm just curious," he told her in a neutral voice that was belied by his very sharp gaze. "The normal curiosity of a man who wants to get to know a lovely woman. Do you realize that all I know about your background is that you're a teacher and that you lived and worked in D.C. before you moved out here?"

"There's nothing else to know."

He lifted an eyebrow, which made him look even more like a warlock.

Josie debated briefly, then shrugged. And when she spoke, it was calmly but rapidly, offering him no opportunity to ask questions. "All right. I was an only child, born to parents who'd given up on having children until I surprised them. My father died ten years ago. My mother left fifteen years ago. I may have a few cousins scattered about, but for all intents and purposes I have no family.

"I like music, the theater, and movies—particularly old ones, and if most of my books weren't in storage, I'm sure you'd be impressed by the size and variety of my library. I love cats, which you know, and am also fond of horses and dogs in that order. Like you, I can cook and sew on a button, and I could even knit you a sweater if I felt so inclined. I can't overhaul an engine, but I can change a tire and check the oil, which is all I've ever needed. My favorite color is blue, my politics are mostly liberal, and if it matters to you, I'm a Scorpio—so don't mess with me if I'm in a bad mood."

Marc was smiling.

Josie went on stolidly. "My first boyfriend gave me my first kiss around the age of nine, as I recall; he did it on a dare, and I was curious, but our teeth got in the way, so neither of us enjoyed the experience. Needless to say, the relationship didn't last. Over the next few years I had several more boyfriends; at that stage, we mostly punched each other on the arm as gestures of affection. In junior high I reached the hand-holding-in-public stage with a boyfriend who knew how to kiss without getting our braces locked; we went steady for more than a year and pretty much fought like two cats tied up in a bag."

When she paused, Marc murmured, "Don't stop now. I've a feeling we're just getting to the interesting part."

She frowned at him. "Not really. I had the

same boyfriend all through high school, but he ended up at Stanford while I went to Wellesley, and neither of us could commute—so that took care of that. I dated in college, but nothing serious. Since then, I've been working long hours, so there hasn't been a lot of time for a social life. And that brings us up to the present."

Marc nodded gravely and leaned over to place his cup on the coffee table. He seemed thoughtful, and when he leaned back and met her gaze, there was a heavy-lidded look to his eyes. It was unmistakably sensual. That was the only warning Josie had before he closed the distance between them, slid his unencumbered right hand under her loose hair to the nape of her neck, and pulled her slowly toward him.

"There's something I have to know," he murmured.

In the seconds granted to her, Josie knew she could stop this. She *knew* she could. All she had to do was stiffen, or pull away, or just say no. No, don't do that. No, I don't want to.

Except that she did want to.

She gazed into his heavy-lidded, tarnished-silver eyes until his lips touched hers, and then she closed her own eyes as an abrupt wave of dizzying pleasure washed over her. His mouth was warm, soft and hard at the same time, and incredibly erotic. She could feel the tension of wariness seeping out of her, feel her body soften and begin to tremble.

She wanted to reach out to him, touch him, but her mind was still too wary for that even if another part of her wasn't. She couldn't reach out. But she couldn't pull back, either, or deny even to herself the pleasure she felt and the overwhelming response of her body to his touch.

She felt the tip of his tongue probing, sliding along the sensitive inner surface of her lip, and a hot shiver rippled through her. She had never felt anything like it before, and was astonished to realize that it was desire. She had believed she'd felt desire before, but now she knew better.

This was desire, swift, hot, and urgent, and everything in her recognized the enormity of it.

Josie didn't know what she might have done if he hadn't drawn slowly away just then, because with that devastating desire had come a confused jumble of emotions she very badly needed to sort through and understand.

"Our teeth didn't get in the way," Marc murmured huskily as he drew back, "and there are no braces to lock, but I have to know how I stack up against your previous boyfriends. It's a macho thing, I'm afraid. The battle of conquest, and all that. So tell me—how do I compare?"

She blinked at him. "What?"

"As a kisser." He appeared perfectly serious.

Josie had a vague objection. "But you aren't my boyfriend."

"We're a little old for the terminology," he agreed. "How does *lover* strike you?"

After a brief moment of uncertainty, Josie got hold of herself. "I don't want a lover, thank you very much," she told him politely.

"No?"

"No." She wished somewhat desperately that she sounded more certain of that. Before Marc could pounce on her hesitancy, she drew away from the fingers lightly stroking her cheek and got up off the couch. "Now, if you don't mind, I've had a long day and I think I'll go home. Thank you for dinner, it was lovely."

He followed her into the kitchen as she headed for the back door and her path across the garden. "I'll walk you to the house," he offered.

"That isn't necessary," she told him as she opened the door. She had the unnerving feeling that he knew very well she was more or less bolting in panic.

"I insist," he said, following her out onto the porch.

"No, Marc, I'll be fine." She went down the steps, relieved when he didn't follow.

Sounding amused, he said, "Well, all right. But you didn't answer my first question."

Josie paused before taking the narrow path that would lead her home, and looked back at him. It was too dark to see him, especially with the light from the kitchen behind him, and his silhouette was so starkly masculine that her throat tightened up in response.

What had he asked? Oh, yes, of course—how

he compared to her "previous boyfriends" as a kisser.

She wanted to lie about it, but although she could evade the truth when necessary, an outright lie was beyond her. Drawing a deep breath, she said, "A-plus. Dammit."

He had a nice laugh. But it didn't do much for her peace of mind to have it echo after her as she bolted home.

Pendragon had apparently found a way into the house, because he was waiting for her inside. Josie didn't know how he'd managed it, but made a mental note to herself to find out in the morning. At the moment she was tired and upset, and the idea of a nice long bath and an early night sounded terrific.

She made sure everything was locked up downstairs, then went up to the bathroom across the hall from her bedroom and began running water into the wonderfully deep claw-footed tub. The cat perched on the rim and watched the scented water rising, intent, and she wondered vaguely if he was the kind of cat who actually liked water.

That idle thought followed her back into her bedroom. She went to the dresser to find a fresh nightgown, and frowned when she saw the key lying there. Marc must have gotten her more rattled than she thought, she decided, because she could have sworn she'd left the key hanging on a hook in the kitchen, well out of Pendragon's reach.

Carrying her nightgown, she started to leave the bedroom—and stopped dead in the doorway. The upstairs hall was fairly dim with only the light from the bathroom and her nightstand lamp illuminating it, but she saw him clearly as he stood at the head of the stairs.

For an instant she thought it was Marc, but then she realized that this man's face was harsher, his eyes lighter. He had the same raven hair, widow's peak, and flying brows, though, and the same tall, powerful build.

And he was looking at her.

Josie couldn't move. She wanted to cry out, but couldn't make a sound. All she could do was stand there, frozen, and wonder wildly how he'd managed to get into the house.

Then she felt a cold, cold finger glide up her spine, when the man held out a hand to her as if pleading for something . . . and Josie realized that he wasn't really there. He couldn't be, because the hand he held out was insubstantial and she could almost see through it.

"Yahhh?"

She jumped almost out of her skin, her eyes skittering from the visitor to where Pendragon stood in the doorway of the bathroom. The big cat wasn't looking at her, he was gazing at the head of the stairs, obviously greeting someone because he was a friendly, responsive cat.

Josie followed his gaze, afraid to see the man there, and more afraid not to.

He was gone.

It took her several minutes to get up the courage, but she finally went through the house from room to room, turning on lights and checking closets, her gun in hand.

Every door she had locked earlier was still firmly latched, dead bolts fastened. All the windows were secure. There was no sign whatsoever that anyone was—or had been—in the house with her and the cat.

No one living, that is.

THREE

Josie didn't expect to get very much sleep that night after the unnerving encounter, but her body had other ideas. Though she was wary enough to lock her bedroom door and leave the lamp on her nightstand on, and had her automatic underneath her pillow—for all the protection any of that would provide against a ghost—she slept soundly from eleven that night until seven the next morning.

In the bright light of a sunny morning, what had happened the night before seemed even more incredible, and she couldn't help wondering if she'd imagined the whole thing. A ghost? Surely not. Though she hadn't been adamant about it, she had never really believed in the supernatural, and she felt a bit silly now when she considered the possibility.

Certainly too silly to mention what she must

have imagined to Marc. Besides, he had specifically said this house wasn't haunted, and he should know after spending so much time here.

With that reassurance in her mind, she was able to shrug off what had probably not even happened the night before. After dressing in her usual casual jeans and a sweater, she went downstairs, and was surprised to find Pendragon sitting on one of the kitchen stools waiting for her. He didn't want out, he wanted breakfast. Josie fed him another can of tuna—her last one—and made a mental note to go to the store for cat food.

Then, while her coffee perked, she searched the house methodically until she found what she was looking for. The cat had been getting in and out on his own since yesterday, so he'd obviously found an open window or some other doorway; Josie didn't much like the idea of that.

But when she found it, relief replaced misgivings. Pendragon had discovered an actual pet door, one that seemed to have been created before such things had become readily available in pet stores. It was in one of the smaller side rooms, maybe a parlor or sitting room originally and one that Josie hadn't explored. A set of multipaned French doors opened out onto the porch, and at the bottom of one of the doors a pane of glass had been reset within a narrow frame and hinged to provide a virtually invisible access door for small pets. The glass was tinted a very faint rose color, presumably so that pets wouldn't forget there was a barrier.

There was a tiny but sturdy sliding bolt that locked the door from the inside; it was so small, it would be easily overlooked, she thought, and it was no wonder she'd missed seeing it.

With the rueful hope that no raccoon or other small forest creature would come exploring, Josie left the pet door unlatched and returned to the kitchen. She poured herself a cup of coffee and, sipping it, idly opened the back door. The morning air was cool rather than cold, but she hardly noticed that because of what she saw through the screen door.

Marc had returned the thermos she'd forgotten the night before; he had probably brought it over before beginning his morning walk. It was sitting on the porch railing beside the steps, with a bright purple ribbon wrapped around it and tied in a jaunty bow; the ribbon rather clashed with the black, red, and yellow plaid in which the thermos was done, but the result was colorful and charming.

Josie stepped out onto the porch and retrieved the thermos. She took it back into the kitchen and, smiling, untied the purple ribbon. A nice touch, she decided. She was about to find a place in one of the cabinets for the thermos, but hesitated.

The previous night's possible ghostly encounter had occupied her thoughts and kept her from thinking very much about Marc and how he'd made her feel. But now there was nothing to distract her, and the memory of his touch was suddenly so vivid that she felt heat sweep up her throat to color her cheeks. Her heart seemed to be beating harder, and she could have sworn that her lips were actually throbbing.

"Good Lord," she muttered. What on earth was wrong with her? She couldn't recall ever having reacted this strongly even to the actual touch of another man—and certainly not to the mere memory of his touch.

With an effort, Josie shook off the sensations. And the ridiculous thoughts. After all, it made perfect sense if she considered the matter logically. In her present state of mind—unusually intense, highly conscious of her feelings of aloneness, and more than a little anxious—she was bound to react strongly to most any new element in her life. And as for the stunningly powerful response to Marc, after long weeks of convalescence, he had doubtless stored up so much sexual energy, it was practically radiating from his body.

No wonder her first impression of him had been so positive. With the combination of pent-up sexual intensity and extraordinary good looks, he could probably seduce a marble statue.

Josie found herself smiling again, and shook her head ruefully. Enough of this. She was being absurd, and that was all there was to it. Marc was her landlord and her neighbor; last night's kiss had been in the nature of an experiment—he had, after all, said as much—and that was as far as it would go. All she had to do was be distantly friendly and make it clear she had come out here for solitude.

Simple enough.

Again, she started to put the thermos up in one of the cabinets, and again she stopped and gazed at it, this time thoughtfully. Well . . . distant but neighborly. Surely there was nothing wrong in being a good neighbor.

"Should I?" she asked Pendragon, who was sitting on a stool washing paws and face after his breakfast.

"Yaahh," he replied promptly and definitely, holding one paw suspended as he looked at her.

She couldn't help laughing, but Josie found herself filling the thermos once again with hot, fragrant coffee. Ruefully aware that she might well be setting a dangerous precedent but shrugging off the possibility with a peculiar sense of defiance, she stuck a note to the thermos that said she had to make a trip to the store for groceries this afternoon, and if Marc needed anything, he should let her know.

As she had the day before, she took the coffee across the garden to the cottage and left it hanging on his doorknob, then returned to the house. She made her own shopping list while she ate toast with apple butter for breakfast and listened absently to the radio.

Finished with her meal and the list, she straightened the kitchen and put the list into her shoulder bag, which she left on the breakfast bar.

She was just about to go into the front parlor and begin the mammoth task of organizing the jumble of files and papers into something approaching a system when her gaze fell on something she hadn't noticed before: a simple little cup hook just to the left of the cellar door.

Pendragon's key was hanging there.

For a moment Josie felt oddly suspended as she stared at it. That key had been lying on her dresser last night . . . though she wasn't at all sure how it had gotten *there*. She had noticed it this morning while brushing her hair, and had left it there in the bedroom. She was positive she had left it there. So how on earth had it gotten down here? The hook was at her eye level, which meant the cat could not have hung the key there even if he'd wanted to.

She went over and lifted the key from its hook, and studied it as it lay in the palm of her hand. Small, old-fashioned key of tarnished brass, faded ribbon. Yes, definitely Pendragon's key. She half turned and regarded the cat, who was still sitting on his stool. He had finished his morning ablutions and returned her gaze with his usual serenity.

"I don't suppose you hung this here?"

The cat tilted his head a bit in a very unfeline gesture, then made a throaty little cooing sound.

Josie wished she spoke cat, because she had the unsettling idea that Pendragon had just told her something important. Pushing *that* ridiculous thought out of her mind, she opened the cellar

door and reached to flick the switch so the bare
bulb at the foot of the stairs glowed to light. Then
she paused and looked back at the cat.

"You do realize I'm only doing this because
I'm not ready to face all that stuff in the front parlor, don't you?"

"Yaah," he responded very softly.

Josie didn't *really* believe the cat had been plac-
ing the key where she couldn't help but see it; in
fact, she would have preferred thinking a ghost
had done it. But even if she herself had subcon-
sciously moved the thing—which was, naturally,
the only thing that could have happened—it was
probably a good idea to find out where it had
come from and put it back.

That was all, of course.

Since the light in the cellar wasn't all that
good, she got her flashlight and carried it down
with her, tucking the brass key into her back
pocket. For a moment she just stood looking
around. The place seemed a little eerie, but she
told herself that was only because it was so dark
and so crammed with boxes and odd-shaped piles
of things. There was certainly nothing unusual or
supernatural down here, just the forgotten possessions of a family.

Even with that reassuring thought, she felt
more than a little jumpy, but forced herself to begin methodically searching among the jumble of
boxes, crates, and old furniture. There were re-
markably few cobwebs, and no signs of bugs or

mice, which was a definite relief since she didn't like either. And Josie didn't have to open anything, after all; Pendragon must have found the key hanging from a box or hook, something like that. All she wanted to do was find out where it belonged.

It couldn't have been much more than ten minutes later, when she'd been distracted by a stack of paintings leaning against the wall and draped with canvas, that a hail from upstairs made her jump.

"Hello?"

"Down here," she called, recognizing Marc's voice instantly. Leaving the paintings still covered, she began making her way through the clutter toward the stairs.

He met her at the bottom. "Hi. Sorry to just barge in, but the back door was open—"

"It's all right," Josie reassured him. "Was there something you needed?" Realizing belatedly how that question might sound, she felt a tide of heat rise in her face. But Marc either found no reason to comment or chose to pass it up.

"Yeah, I wanted to take you up on your offer and ask you to get a few things for me when you do your shopping this afternoon," he replied easily. Then he peered past the circle of light where they stood, and added, "Why is it so dark down here?"

"Because it's a cellar."

"Funny." He reached over to a light switch

Josie hadn't seen on the wall near them and flipped it a couple of times. When nothing happened, he took the flashlight from her hand and made his way toward the switch box, saying over his shoulder, "When the place was rewired, I added more lights in a few places, including here. That switch should be on. . . ." He opened the switch box and aimed the flashlight in. "But it isn't."

Josie blinked as the click of a switch being thrown was followed by generous light. Now illuminated by three more simple, bare-bulb fixtures, the cellar appeared relatively neat and certainly innocent, and Josie felt a little foolish when she remembered her earlier thoughts.

"This is much better, thanks," she said as Marc rejoined her.

"My pleasure." He turned off the flashlight and set it on the fourth tread of the stairs. "So you decided to explore down here after all?"

"Sort of. That key Pendragon found is beginning to bother me."

"Oh? Why?"

Josie started to tell him about the key turning up in places where she hadn't left it, but chickened out. She really didn't want to admit to something that sounded so odd, especially when she wasn't a hundred percent sure she hadn't moved the key herself. So, instead, she merely said, "I guess I'm more curious than I thought I was. You don't mind?"

"Mind your exploring? Of course not, Josie, I told you that. As a matter of fact, if you'd like some company, I wouldn't mind looking around down here myself. Lord knows what we'll find, but the search might be fun."

Josie barely hesitated. "Why not? I was planning to spend at least a couple of hours down here before lunch; that should satisfy my curiosity." She told herself she agreed to his suggestion only because she'd feel better about exploring in the presence of the owner of the house, but she didn't believe that rational reasoning.

She showed the key to Marc and explained her thinking on where the cat must have found it, and they began searching different areas of the cellar. For half an hour or so, the search was brisk and they said little to each other beyond brief comments on what they found.

"What is this?"

"An iron. I think."

"For clothes? You're kidding."

"No, and thank heaven for progress; permanent press is wonderful, and so are clothes dryers. A decorator would probably pay you a fortune for that thing—turn it into a cute bookend or something. Country chic."

"Well, there's a whole box of them here. I'll remember if I need some quick cash."

"You do that. Hey—I found a birdhouse. It must have been on that post in the garden. I wonder why they took it down."

"I wonder why they put it down here. My relatives kept the damnedest things. . . . Here's a pair of shears with only one blade. Why keep that?"

"In the days before planned obsolescence, somebody probably meant to repair them. The way they must have meant to fix this two-legged stool."

"For God's sake . . ."

Though ostensibly helping Josie to look for the key's origins, Marc didn't hesitate to open trunks, boxes, and crates "just for the hell of it."

"We have to look for that lost Rembrandt," he told her, peering into an old steamer trunk that held an astonishing variety of peculiar kitchen utensils.

"Yeah, right." But it reminded Josie of the paintings she had been about to look through before he arrived. Abandoning, without much regret, her exploration of shelves full of canned preserves and somebody's rock collection, she made her way back to where the paintings leaned against a wall.

She had to push a box labeled *books* out of her way in order to get to the paintings, and that box came in very handy when she flipped back the canvas and saw the first painting—because she sat down rather suddenly and the box made an adequate seat.

"Marc? Who is this?" Josie thought her voice sounded very peculiar, but he didn't seem to notice anything as he came and knelt beside her.

"That is—or was—Luke Westbrook," he replied. "I'd forgotten there was a painting of him."

It was a good painting, well-done and beautifully lifelike, and the years had done surprisingly little harm to it. Stored in its heavy gilt frame and covered with the canvas, it hadn't even gotten dusty. But that wasn't the reason Josie felt so dazed. She felt dazed because this was the man she had seen at the top of the stairs last night.

He looked enough like Marc to have been an older brother. Features handsome but more rough-hewn. Gleaming black hair with that arresting widow's peak. Striking gray eyes a shade lighter than Marc's—less tarnish and more silver showing through. Painted as a writer would have been earlier in this century, sitting at his desk with a fountain pen in one well-shaped hand and a sheaf of papers before him, wearing suit and tie. A small, slightly off-centered smile curving his lips.

A male Mona Lisa, mysterious and enigmatic.

"Josie?"

She had never seen a picture of Luke Westbrook until this moment; Josie was absolutely sure of that. She'd had no idea that Marc so resembled his kinsman. So—even if she'd taken it into her head to conjure a ghost out of her own imagination, how could she have been so on target?

She turned her head slowly. The light here was especially good, illuminating the painting as well as her and Marc. Still kneeling at her side, Marc was looking at her, frowning. She wondered what her expression was like to cause him to look so concerned.

"Josie, what's wrong?"

"I thought you said this place wasn't haunted."

His eyebrows shot up. "As far as I know, it isn't."

Without taking her gaze off Marc, Josie jerked a thumb toward the painting. "Tell that to him."

Marc shifted so that he was turned toward her, still on one knee. He rested the cast covering his left arm on his raised knee and studied her with a gaze that was very concentrated and not a little unnerving. She decided that just so would he turn his scrutiny into a silver-sheened rapier to skewer a difficult or deceitful witness in the courtroom.

She didn't like it. At all.

Fierce, she said, "I *did not* imagine it! I saw him upstairs, in the hallway, last night—as clearly as I see you now. He might have been a bit transparent, but I *saw* him. Even the cat saw him, for God's sake—"

"All right." His right hand reached out to touch her knee. "I believe you, Josie."

Convinced he was only humoring her, she moved her knee to escape his hand and then rose to her feet. "I'd never seen a ghost in my life until last night," she muttered, picking her way through the clutter to head toward the stairs. "And I've discovered I don't particularly want to share a house with one. I'm telling you now, if he starts rattling chains or doing anything else spooky, I'm out of here." She tried to keep her voice light, but didn't think she quite pulled it off.

Marc followed her across the cellar and turned off the secondary set of lights before going up the stairs, accepting her obvious decree that their exploration was over for the day.

"I thought you didn't scare easily," he said as they emerged into the bright airiness of the kitchen.

Josie might well have fired up at that, but his tone was absentminded rather than provocative, and when she turned to look at him, it was to find him obviously bothered by thoughts darker than simple teasing or mockery.

"Maybe I was wrong about that," she said mildly.

"What was he doing when you saw him?"

Since the question appeared to be serious, Josie replied in a serious tone. "He was standing at the head of the stairs. I had just come out of my bedroom and—and there he was. Just standing there looking at me. I thought it was you at first, but his features were harsher and the clothes weren't right. He seemed anxious, frowning a little. He lifted a hand, his left, almost as if . . ."

"As if?" Marc prompted.

"Well, I got the impression he was . . . asking something. That he wanted something of me." She tried to laugh and knew the sound held little humor. "Then I heard Pendragon speak, the way he does when he's saying hello, and I looked at him. He was standing in the doorway of the bathroom, and he was staring toward the head of the stairs as if he saw somebody. When I nerved myself to look back there . . ."

"The . . . visitor was gone?"

"Yeah. I told myself he couldn't possibly have been a ghost, so I checked every door and window in this house, and nothing was unlocked. Absolutely nothing. There was nobody here but me and the cat."

"I see."

Marc was looking at her so oddly that Josie was convinced he thought she was nuts—a profession of belief in her story notwithstanding—and was seriously considering calling a padded wagon and having her hauled away. She couldn't really blame him, except for the tiny fact that she knew she wasn't crazy. Tension stole through her.

"Look, never mind." She turned away to discover he'd brought back the thermos and set it on the counter. *Just wait and see if I fix him anymore coffee, dammit.* "I probably imagined the whole thing. Do you have a shopping list for me?"

"Josie, I believe you."

She put the thermos into the cabinet with a rather final air and went over to get her purse. "I think I'll go now and get this done—"

"Josie." He put his hands on her shoulders and turned her to face him. "I said I believe you."

He didn't believe her, she was certain of it, and

her tension increased to the point that it actually hurt. On some level of herself, Josie was aware that she was abnormally sensitive to anybody—anybody at all—doubting her word. She had spent too many years watching her father try to convince people he was telling the truth, only to fail time after time and be openly viewed as at best a liar and at worst a callous monster. The experience had destroyed her father, and had left Josie with a painfully heightened awareness of skepticism and disbelief—and a violent reaction to either.

If everyone had a "button," a sore spot deep in the psyche that, if touched, was guaranteed instantly to provoke them beyond reason, being doubted was Josie's.

But being aware of that did nothing at all to control the reaction. Stiff, she moved back away from him until his hands fell, wondering vaguely if her face looked as frozen as it felt. "Skip it," she said flatly. "I'm going shopping now, so if you have a list, hand it over."

He hesitated only a moment, gazing at her with a frown, but then reached into his shirt pocket and produced a folded list and some money. "Just a few things, if you wouldn't mind. Spend whatever's left on Pendragon," he told her, his tone a bit preoccupied. "Cat food, toys—whatever."

"Fine. I should be back in a couple of hours or so."

Instead of returning to the cottage after being so brusquely dismissed by Josie, Marc went only as far as a stone bench in the overgrown garden. He heard her van start up a few minutes later and caught a glimpse of her driving away, and then the quiet day settled over him.

What the hell had just happened?

From a friendly, humorous, and companionable woman enjoying their exploration of the cellar, she had turned into a stiff—no, dammit, *frozen* —woman with eyes that looked through him and a voice as flat as a copper coin run over by a train. Why? Because he hadn't instantly believed that she had actually seen a ghost last night?

Okay, maybe some people were touchy about things like that, but her reaction went far beyond touchy.

Marc leaned forward on the bench and rested his forearms on his knees. He looked up as a hint of motion caught his eye and watched Pendragon stroll down the narrow path toward him. The cat sat down a couple of feet away, tail curled around forepaws, and regarded the man with his faintly crossed and oddly Siamese-blue eyes.

"Yaah," he said softly.

"So you saw the ghost, too, huh, cat?"

His face wearing a permanent cat-smile, Pendragon blinked and made a throaty cooing sound.

Marc frowned at him. "No court I know of

would believe a feline witness—and I have to admit having a few doubts myself, old chum. But, *her* now . . . do I believe her?"

"Yah," Pendragon replied briefly and emphatically.

Throwing off the notion that the cat had actually answered his question, Marc brooded silently. Did he believe in ghosts? No, he didn't think he did believe in them, although he hadn't given the matter much thought until now. Serious thought, that is. As a boy, he had certainly lain awake on more than one summer night listening eagerly for the creak of a ghostly step on a stair tread, but now, as a grown-up lawyer trained in reason and logic as well as the laws of probability, he discounted the idea of spirits wandering through his house.

But he had to admit he'd never before known anyone personally who had had a close encounter with a ghost, and so he had always been able to view the matter with detached objectivity.

Until now. And, even now, he tried to consider the possibility objectively.

Had Josie really seen Luke Westbrook last night? Logic said it was unlikely, even absurd. There were no such things as ghosts, and besides, if Luke had been haunting the house all this time, why hadn't anyone else seen him? As far as Marc knew—and he was pretty sure he would have known if it were otherwise—in the fifty years since his death, nobody had so much as caught a glimpse of Luke. So why suddenly would a complete stranger to the family be the audience of his belated appearance?

Logically, it was doubtful that Josie had really seen the ghost of Luke Westbrook.

Marc was, however, not so wedded to logic that he wasn't willing to suspend his disbelief—provided he saw old Luke himself. Until then, until he was presented with something his own eyes could verify, he knew he wouldn't be able to pretend a belief he didn't feel.

But why had she reacted so strongly to his doubts? Any rational person would expect to face skepticism on the subject of ghostly visitations, after all, and he was reasonably sure Josie was a rational person. Reasonably sure.

So why had she frozen up on him? Why had her reaction been so . . . extreme? He had enough experience dealing with people to feel sure there was a reason; people's strongest reactions tended to spring from the hurts they carried around with them, and those hurts rarely existed without cause. So what—or who—had hurt Josie Douglas?

It was Marc's nature to seek the solution to a puzzle, but with this one he felt an unusual sense of urgency. He hadn't liked being frozen out by Josie, he hadn't liked it at all, and he had no intention of allowing her to go on freezing him out. He told himself it was simply because he disliked being on bad terms with his neighbor/tenant, especially when she was a lovely woman with unusual eyes and a smile that had mysteriously found its way into his dreams last night. . . .

He sat there for a few moments longer gazing toward the big house, frowning. He had the distinct feeling that Josie wasn't going to confide in him and would probably, in fact, continue to freeze him out unless he found a way past that protective shell. Without her help. So . . . how?

He certainly couldn't get into the house while she was gone and look through her stuff for his answers—that would be an inexcusable and unforgivable intrusion even if he could bring himself to do it, which he couldn't.

Marc got up and headed toward the cottage, vaguely aware that Pendragon was accompanying him. His right leg was aching a bit, and he rubbed the upper thigh with the heel of his right hand absently. It was going to rain soon. His doctor—and good friend—had told him that people who'd had bones broken could often literally feel in those bones changes in the weather, and he certainly could.

There was probably some scientific explanation, of course, like the pin in his thigh reacting to a change in barometric pressure or something. Broken bones never knit *precisely*, and the asymmetry probably had something to do with it as well. . . .

Marc shook his head and went into the cottage, automatically holding the door so that the big black cat could come in. Pendragon had already chosen a favorite chair close to the fireplace, and he went immediately to make himself comfortable there. Marc got the portable phone and sat down on the couch. He didn't have to concentrate to remember the number, because it was a familiar one.

"Tucker? Marc."

"Hey, shyster, how're the bones knitting?" Tucker Mackenzie had played cops-and-robbers with Marc when the two had been boys in Richmond, and they were such close friends that any casual listener might have thought them enemies.

"They're knitting just fine, thanks to Neil— and no thanks to you. That jigsaw puzzle you sent nearly drove me out of my mind, and I'd like to know how the hell I was supposed to play that damned video game with my good hand in a cast."

"I was just trying to challenge you," Tucker explained innocently.

"You were trying to drive me crazy."

Tucker chuckled. "It sounds like I succeeded. Is the country exile getting to you?"

"Let's just say that the sounds of traffic would be music to my ears right now. Tucker, I need my car."

"Sorry, chum, but Neil promised to break a few of *my* bones if I gave in to you. When the cast comes off your arm, and not before, you know that."

Marc made a sound of exasperation. "Look,

I'm practically healed—eleven days until the cast comes off—"

"Counting down, I see."

"Tucker."

With another chuckle, Tucker said, "Hey, don't snap at me. Neil is determined to make sure you stay far away from your office or any courtroom, and since he's my doctor as well as yours, I'd rather not upset him. He might do something nasty to me. Typhoid germs or something."

"You have a writer's imagination," Marc told him ruefully.

"Most writers do."

"Yeah, but yours works overtime."

"Which is probably why my books do so well." In a more serious tone, Tucker added, "Aside from helping you escape the wilds of the country, what can I do? If you're worried about your shiny new BMW, don't; it's nice and safe in my garage."

"No, I'm not worried about it, I just *want* it." Marc sighed. "I'd like to know what Neil has on you to make you so obedient to his commands."

Tucker didn't take the bait. "If you need anything, you know I'm available. I happen to be between books at the moment anyway, so I've got time on my hands. So?"

Marc hesitated, but only for an instant. He'd had this in the back of his mind all along, he realized. There was no one he knew who was better than Tucker at digging up information—and he could be counted on for discretion.

"How do you feel about doing a little research for me?" Marc asked slowly.

"You better not be working on a case."

"I'm not. This is something . . . personal."

"Oh, yeah?" There was immediate interest in Tucker's voice. "How personal?"

Marc cleared his throat. "Well, I have a new tenant in the house. She just moved in on Tuesday, and—"

"She?"

"Yes, she. Will you let me finish?"

"Absolutely."

Convalescence made a man touchy, Marc thought defensively, conscious of snapping at his friend once again. "The thing is, I need to have her background checked out."

"Why?"

Marc couldn't think of a single reason he was willing to give to his friend, and so he fell back on a flat and unanswerable response. "Because."

"Um. Is this a young woman, by any chance?"

"Late twenties."

"And attractive, I suppose?"

"Some would consider her . . . pretty." And any man in his right mind would consider that the understatement of the year, Marc reflected silently.

"Uh-huh. Are you worried about her stealing the silver?"

"No."

"Tearing up your house?"

"No."

"Disturbing your peace with wild parties?"

"If she threw a wild party, I'd be the first in line," Marc muttered.

There was a moment of silence, and then Tucker said musingly, "So this is personal. How about that. I've never known you to be so devious in finding out about a woman. The usual procedure, you know, is to ask. Invite her to dinner, make some of your legendary spaghetti sauce, ply her with wine."

"Yeah, well, I somehow doubt that would work."

"Already tried it, huh?"

Marc sighed. "Tucker, must I remind you that my patience is worn a bit thin these days?"

"All right, all right, I was just asking. Obviously, this lady requires a more delicate touch. So you want me to do a little research into her life. Fine, I'd be glad to. What am I looking for? Hobbies you can discuss with her? Political affiliations? A criminal record?"

"I don't know, dammit." Marc hesitated, then said, "Look, there's just something . . . off center. I've dealt with enough witnesses to know when somebody is hiding something—and she is. She seems very reluctant to discuss her background, for one thing. And when I doubted something she'd said, she went into a deep freeze so fast I nearly got frostbitten."

"Sounds like an interesting lady."

Warningly, Marc said, "I don't want you coming out here, Tucker."

"You're hurting my feelings. Why not?"

"Because you're predatory."

"I resent that."

"I imagine you might, but it's the truth. The last time I introduced you to a lady, she broke a date with me to accompany you to the racetrack."

"My fatal charm. She was wrong for you anyway. Come to think of it, she was wrong for me too."

Their mostly good-natured competition over women had been going on since junior high, and though there had been one actual fight that Marc could remember, the contest generally ended with the amicable concession of one or the other. To date, the honors were fairly equally divided between them.

Marc was a bit surprised at himself now to realize that he definitely did *not* want Tucker anywhere near Josie.

FOUR

Tucker was surprised as well—and thoughtful.

"So you want the lady all to yourself, huh?"

"I didn't say that."

"Yes, you did." Before Marc could retort, Tucker went on cheerfully. "Okay, give me her particulars. Name, age, height and coloring, measurements, her car's tag number, if you know it. Stuff like that."

"Her name's Josie Douglas; I have no idea if Josie is short for Josephine, and I don't know if that's her first or her middle name. She's twenty-eight. About five-foot-five and very slender. Red hair, violet eyes."

"Violet?" Tucker asked in surprise.

"Yeah."

"Unusual. Measurements?"

"Forget it, Tucker."

"Well, can't blame a man for trying." Tucker

laughed. "Did you happen to get a look at her car tag?"

Marc, who had an almost uncanny memory for numbers, rattled off the tag number of Josie's van and described the vehicle. "I don't know much more," he said. "She says she's an elementary teacher taking a year off to try and write."

"That sounds like *I'd* have more in common with her than—"

"Forget it, Tucker."

"I was just making an observation."

"I know what you were just doing. Forget it. If you show up out here, I'll tell Josie you're an ex-felon I helped put away years ago."

"You're a defense attorney."

"In order to get my client off, I found out and was able to prove you'd done it."

"Done what?"

Exasperated, Marc said, "I'll think of something dire. And I'll make her believe it."

"Ummm. I suppose you would, at that."

"Can we get back to the point, please?"

"Sure we can. You were telling me what you knew about Josie. She's taken a year off to try and write, and . . . ?"

"And she used to live and teach in D.C., although I don't know if she was born there. Father died about ten years ago, mother left about five years before that. No siblings. Oh, and she went to Wellesley."

"The spaghetti must have worked a little,"

Tucker noted dryly, "since you do know a few things about her."

Marc ignored the comment. "How long do you think it'll take you to find out anything?"

"Oh, hell, at least a few days. Maybe even a week or two. Thanks to one of my hacker friends, I can tap into a few data banks most people don't have access to, but even with the computer it's going to take a little time, Marc."

"Will you call me as soon as you have something?"

"Sure."

"Thanks, Tucker."

"Don't thank me yet—I might not be able to find out any more than you already know. But I'll try. And if you don't mind a bit of advice from an old friend—or even if you do—you might try to forget you're a lawyer when you're with the lady, okay? She might not like being on the witness stand."

"I never—"

"Sure you do. You always do. Bye, Marc."

He listened to the dial tone for a moment, then turned the phone off and set it on the end table, frowning. *Did* he tend to pounce on people, automatically probing for the truth even in a casual situation? It was an unsettling possibility.

Resolving to try to watch that, Marc turned his attention to the problem of Josie. The problem of how to get closer to Josie. His intuition told him that if he pressed her to confide in him before she was ready to do so, she would simply fold up her tent and leave; she didn't trust him. In fact, a reluctance to trust anybody might well turn out to be one of her problems, and only time and knowledge would prove to her that he was trustworthy.

So he would have to walk a fine line, refusing to be frozen out while at the same time fighting his instincts to dig for the truth.

Great.

He looked down at his left arm, absently flexing his fingers. Maybe being forced into patience was a good thing, he thought. With this awkward plaster weighing him down, he felt like a bird with a broken wing, and no man liked to feel that way with a lovely woman about—unless, of course, he wanted to appeal to her maternal instinct.

Marc grimaced. No. The last thing he wanted from Josie was mothering.

So—in eleven days, the cast would be off and he'd be virtually back to normal. Sometime during those eleven days, Tucker would probably have at least some information about Josie's background, information that Marc could use to get through her frozen shell.

She was not going to like finding out that he'd had her background researched, he knew that. But he wasn't doing anything unscrupulous, he told himself, since whatever information Tucker found —most of it anyway—would be a matter of public record, available to anyone who wanted to look for it. And it wasn't as if he meant in any way to hurt her or shout her secrets to the world. No, he only wanted to understand.

Already rehearsing my defense. That alone told him he wasn't comfortable with what he was doing —but he couldn't pull back now. Having once chosen a particular course, Marc tended to stick with it all the way.

He looked up to find the big black cat watching him intently with Siamese eyes, and almost unconsciously spoke aloud to his feline companion.

"I have a feeling I'm going to risk frostbite again unless I can convince her I don't believe she imagined seeing the ghost of my illustrious ancestor. So . . . how do I convince *myself* that she could have seen him? I don't believe in ghosts."

"Yaaah," Pendragon commented succinctly.

"Well, that's probably excellent advice, but I don't happen to speak cat," Marc told him dryly.

Pendragon uttered a throaty murmur and jumped down from his chair. He stretched languidly, unexpectedly distinct muscles rippling under the glossy black coat, then yawned. He looked at Marc for a moment, then abruptly pounced on nothing at all and began to play with it.

Marc had observed other cats chasing figments of their imaginations, a pastime that seemed to provide exercise as well as entertainment, and he watched Pendragon absently as the cat batted his invisible prize here and there. Around a leg of the coffee table, under a chair, even bounding over the couch in an athletic leap, Pendragon happily chased his figment. He cornered it at the book-shelves by the window, and a moment later a thud announced that in wrestling with his figment, he had somehow dislodged a book.

Curious, Marc went to see, and found the cat innocently washing a forepaw with his other one planted firmly on the book lying on the floor. Nothing else on the shelf had been disturbed, and Marc frowned as he bent down and picked up the book.

It was an old book, long out of print, since it had been published in the forties. It was a biography of Luke Westbrook, the only one in existence that had been written by someone who had actually known the mystery writer; Marc knew of the book, even though he'd never read it.

It also happened to be the only book about Luke Westbrook on the shelf—and in the cottage.

"Coincidence," Marc heard himself say in a rather peculiar tone. "Pure coincidence." He looked at the cat, who uttered another of those throaty murmurs of his and then went placidly back to his favorite chair.

Marc returned to his own place on the couch, holding the book and gazing between it and Pendragon. It had to be a coincidence, of course. As much as he loved and appreciated cats, and as much as he would have liked to believe they were unusually intelligent creatures, he didn't think they could read *or* suggest solutions to human problems—even if they understood said problems, which was doubtful.

Still . . . He looked at the book, shrugged, and opened it. God knew he had time on his hands. And maybe he'd find something useful. Maybe. At the very least he owed it to his ancestor to know all the facts. . . .

It was quite some time later when Marc was roused by an imperative demand from Pendragon. The cat waited until his human companion marked his place and laid the book aside, then repeated his demand and went briskly to the door. Obediently, Marc followed him and opened the door for him.

The crunch of tires on gravel reached his ears as Marc stepped out onto the porch, and he looked down at the cat thoughtfully. "So that's why you wanted out, because she's home."

"Yaaah." Pendragon stood looking up at him, waiting so obviously that he might as well have been tapping an impatient paw.

"She doesn't want to see me," he told the cat.

"Yaaah," Pendragon repeated in the same commanding tone.

"I should help with the groceries, I know, and there's my stuff to bring over, but . . ." He frowned down at the cat. "Why am I discussing this with you?"

"Ppprupt."

"No doubt." Marc looked across the garden toward the house. His aching bones hadn't been wrong; the afternoon had turned gray and very damp, with the smell of rain in the air. He hesitated a moment longer, then shrugged and headed across the garden, following behind Pendragon as the cat led the way. All he could do, he decided, was gauge Josie's mood and behave accordingly; if she had thawed or had second thoughts during the shopping trip, great, and if she was still freezing him, he'd do his best to chip away at the ice without pressing too hard.

As easy as walking a highwire. Without a net.

For just an instant, as he considered the task ahead of him, Marc thought there was actually a lot to be said for the peace and quiet and lack of undue complications of being completely alone out here—but then he caught sight of Josie. And seeing her, he suddenly felt a jolt of all his senses that was becoming a familiar sensation.

He had felt it the first time he had seen her, the sensations so strong and unexpected that he had been instantly wary of them. His imagination, surely; it had to be. He told himself each time that he wouldn't feel it again, not again, but each time he saw her he felt it. Like an electric shock that left him acutely alive and aware, his heart beating faster and his breathing somehow more difficult than it had been.

There was a part of him that didn't want to be wary of it, a part already fascinated by and absorbed in her. *Do you feel this too? Have you ever felt it before? Please say you feel it too. Because it would be the most painful thing in the world to feel this alone, I think. . . .*

But he couldn't say that to Josie, of course. She'd think he was crazy, or else handing her a line—and either way her likely response would be a hasty retreat, possibly faster and farther than he could go in pursuit.

So he hid what he felt under a calm surface. His courtroom experience had taught him to master whatever he felt, to control body language and inflection, and by now he was able to do so automatically, even outside a courtroom. Without even thinking about it, he made himself low-key and unthreatening, casual and friendly without stepping over the line she had drawn between them. As if he had never held her in his arms.

"Hi. I came to help."

"I could have managed." Her voice was calm, not so frozen as before, but definitely cool.

"I know, but since you did my shopping as well, it's the least I could do." He gathered a couple of grocery bags from the van and followed her into the house. Once in the kitchen, she immediately began putting things away while he returned to the van for the last of the bags.

"It's raining," he reported as he rejoined her in the kitchen and set the bags on the counter. "Sort of, anyway. More of an enthusiastic mist than anything else."

"According to the weather reports," Josie said, "it's going to rain until Sunday."

"Miserable weather, good only for staying in-doors. All the fireplaces are in good shape, if you want to build a fire," Marc told her. "And there's plenty of extra wood stacked by the back porch, in case you didn't see it."

"I saw it, thanks. You didn't say how much milk, so I got you a gallon—is that okay?"

"Fine . . ."

The conversation went on, casual and inconse-quential, both of them being just polite enough to make the effort obvious. Josie finished putting away her groceries and separated Marc's into a couple of bags on the counter. He opened a pack-age containing a catnip mouse and enticed Pen-dragon, who showed himself to be a normal feline when it came to catnip and soon happily carried his treat away to play with it by himself.

"Have you had lunch?" Josie asked.

Marc looked at his watch, surprised to find that it was after two. "As a matter of fact, I forgot all about it. I've been . . . reading."

Josie was putting a pot on the stove and didn't look at him. "I'm having soup, I think. Would you like some?"

Not about to pass up any invitation, he said, "I'd love some, thanks."

"Then why don't you take your groceries over and put them away, and by the time you get back, the soup should be ready," she suggested.

"Sounds good to me."

Josie held the door for him, then stood there

watching until he vanished into the cottage. She closed the door and began opening cans of thick, rich soup.

It had turned into a good day for soup, gray and dreary with the temperature chilly enough to make things miserable without being cold enough for snow or sleet . . . and why had she invited Marc for a belated lunch?

As a tacit apology, dammit.

The methodical task of shopping had calmed her somewhat, leaving her guiltily conscious of having overreacted to his skepticism. After all, she'd realized, it *was* a ghost they'd been talking about, something that was, by definition, a thing difficult to believe—even if you saw it with your own eyes. To be perfectly honest, she admitted reluctantly, if he had been the one to tell her he'd seen a ghost, she probably would have been a bit skeptical herself.

More than a bit, actually.

She couldn't throw stones. Besides that, what did it matter? So he didn't believe she'd really seen a ghost—so what? She probably hadn't seen it. She'd been tired, the upstairs hall had been shadowy, and he'd looked like Marc because Marc was on her mind, not because what she'd seen was—or had been—Luke Westbrook. . . .

Josie shook her head and put the coffee on, and then began assembling ingredients for sandwiches while the soup bubbled. And even if she *had* seen a real ghost—so what? It was certainly no big deal.

In seeing a ghost, she had joined the ranks of those who had experienced some paranormal encounter, without rhyme or reason, probably a once-in-a-lifetime thing, and there was no reason to fret about it.

But she couldn't help fretting, because the circumstances struck her as odd. Marc's reaction told her that the house didn't have the reputation of being haunted, and one would wonder why Luke Westbrook chose to pop up now, fifty years after his death.

Unless . . . he had appeared before but only at specific times during which the house happened to be empty. Like maybe . . . the anniversary of his death? Wasn't that supposedly a reason ghosts appeared? He'd suffered a violent death, even if self-inflicted, and perhaps the anniversary of that death demanded his presence in the world of the living. If this place had mostly been used as a summer house, then it was possible no one had been in residence at this time of year, and if Luke Westbrook had died in the fall . . .

When Marc knocked on the door a few minutes later, she opened it and immediately asked, "When did Luke Westbrook die? The month and day, I mean."

Without a blink, Marc replied, "April fifteenth. I've always remembered because of taxes."

Discouraged, Josie retreated to the stove to stir the soup.

"I thought of that too," Marc said as he leaned back against the breakfast bar.

"Thought of what?" she murmured, self-conscious.

"Why Luke might suddenly have appeared now after all these years."

She turned her head and eyed him. "You don't believe he did appear."

Marc smiled faintly. "I'm trying to be open-minded about it. Look, Josie, I've never believed in ghosts. But I believe *you* believe you saw something last night. So . . . I've been thinking about it. As far as I know, he's never appeared in the house at all in fifty years, and even though the place hasn't been occupied steadily, there have been people here most summers and even a few winters."

Sighing, Josie said, "Pour yourself some coffee and have a seat. The soup's done."

Marc fixed coffee for them both and set the cups on the bar, where a plate of sandwiches covered by a napkin waited. Josie dished up the soup, and they ate sitting at right angles to each other at the bar. For a while neither said anything beyond the normal pleasantries of commenting on how good the soup was or requesting that the salt be passed, but when they were finishing up the meal, Marc spoke thoughtfully.

"Have you ever had an experience with the paranormal? Before last night, I mean."

"I'm not even unusually intuitive," she replied,

glad that their careful politeness with each other had passed. "You know that experiment that's supposed to test psychic ability—the one with the cards with all the symbols on them?"

"Square, circle, wavy lines—like that?"

"Right. In college, some friends and I duplicated that experiment and tested each other. My score was well below what I should have guessed right out of sheer dumb luck. I wasn't even as good as the law of averages."

Marc sipped his coffee, then mused, "I seem to remember reading somewhere that an unusually low score on that test might actually indicate psychic ability."

"Really?" Josie thought about it, then shook her head. "In my case, I doubt that's true. I haven't even had a glimmer of anything paranormal in my life. Not even lucky hunches or expecting the phone to ring before it does."

"So why would the ghost of my ancestor suddenly appear before you?" Marc kept his voice thoughtful, considering, and made certain there was no hint of disbelief in his tone.

"Beats the hell out of me. Since I'm obviously not psychic, it isn't because I'm sensitive to the paranormal. The only connection I have to him is the fact that I'm here in his house, and I don't even know much about him beyond the fact that he wrote books I happen to enjoy reading. This isn't the anniversary of his death." She brooded. "What about his birth date?"

Marc half closed his eyes in thought. "Ummm. July, I think. Around the fourth."

"Scratch that." Josie sipped her coffee and continued to brood. "I don't suppose you knocked out any walls or unsealed any rooms while you were renovating?"

Startled, Marc said, "Definitely no sealed rooms. But even if we had found one—he died in the front parlor, remember? And he's buried in the family plot between here and Richmond. There's no question about either of those facts. So his—his spirit could hardly have been trapped here in the house by some physical barrier, if that's what you're getting at."

"For somebody who doesn't believe in ghosts," she noted neutrally, "you seem to know all about them."

He shook his head. "When I was a kid, as I told you, my cousins and I used to hope this place was haunted, and we often scared ourselves silly telling stories. I also have a good friend with a wide range of interests who happened to get on a paranormal kick a few years ago, and he told me a few things."

"Things you didn't believe?"

"Well, eventually he invited me to attend a sé-ance he held one Halloween night. After that, I sort of took everything he said with a grain of dis-belief."

Solemn, Josie said, "I gather the spirits weren't in a talkative mood?"

"Apparently." Marc had never quite gotten over the notion that his friend had arranged the whole damn thing just to pull his leg, but Tucker *swore* . . . "So, anyway, I've picked up a few of the most widely accepted precepts of haunting. Like the importance of anniversaries and the significance of sealed rooms. But neither of those seems to apply here."

Josie shook her head. "And we still come back to *why now*. Fifty years since his death . . . and why now does he suddenly appear? Look, as far as I can see, only two things are different about the house at the moment. You renovated recently, and I moved in. I don't see how it could be me—so it has to be something that was done to the house. Don't you think?"

Whether or not he believed in ghosts, Marc had always enjoyed puzzles, and this was a good one. "Well, I have to admit I don't see another possibility, at least not so far. But the renovations were pretty basic, you know. The general structure of the house wasn't changed. The kitchen was redone, expanded, but the extra space came from a large pantry and closet that were unnecessary. New heating and updated wiring, so there was some work done in the walls—but if the workmen found anything, they didn't let me know about it.

"The chimneys were swept, fireplaces sandblasted. The floors were refinished, and a lot of the woodwork stripped and refinished. New windows and shingles. Paint. That's about it."

"Is the furniture original?" Josie asked.

"You mean from the forties? Not much of it, no. Some of the small tables, I think. That settee in the side parlor, and the secretary in the front parlor, I'm pretty sure. Oh—and everything in the largest bedroom."

Her bedroom. "You mean all that stuff belonged to Luke?"

"Yeah, it was his bedroom. The furniture was really good—solid and heavy, well-made—so it's lasted."

"Maybe that was why he was holding up his hand," Josie noted wryly. "Telling me to get out of his bedroom."

Marc frowned. "Was he commanding—or asking? You said he held his hand out as if he wanted something of you."

She thought about it, then nodded. "Asking. At least that's the way it seemed to me. It was almost . . . pleading, that gesture. And there was something about his expression that really got to me. He seemed so anxious, so troubled about something."

"But we don't know what that something is."

"No, we don't." Josie slid off her stool and went to open the dishwasher. "And unless I find some ghostly writing on a mirror somewhere, or some other hint to explain what's going on, I don't see how we can know."

Marc got up to help clear away the remains of their meal, and for a little while they were silent, both absently saying hello to Pendragon when the cat leaped up on a stool and greeted them politely.

Then Marc said, "I wouldn't blame you a bit if you were uneasy about staying here now. Are you?"

Josie shrugged. "No, I don't think so. It was definitely a spooky experience, but I'm not afraid anything's going to happen to me. I just wish I could figure out why I saw him, and what he wants of me."

"These Westbrook men," Marc said lightly, as if it didn't mean anything. "Appearing suddenly in your life and . . . demanding something of you. Maybe you just fascinate us."

"You haven't demanded anything," she heard herself say in an amazingly casual tone.

"I don't want to. To demand, that is. But I am glad you've appeared suddenly in *my* life."

Josie tamed the leap of her heart, and as she closed the loaded dishwasher with a firm hand, she managed to keep her voice dry and calm. "Luke's dead and you're bored—that might account for it. You've both been alone too long."

"I can't argue with your assessment of him," Marc said, "but I will defend myself. Bored I have certainly been, but nobody's ever accused me of not knowing my own mind."

Josie wished the cleaning-up hadn't gone so fast; she badly needed something to do with her hands. Grabbing a dishrag, she began wiping the counter. "Even a smart man might be driven to do something dumb if he'd spent too much time alone," she observed in a determinedly offhand tone.

"That might well be true. But I haven't spent too much time alone; I have several friends who've visited regularly, and I've been fairly well occupied —no matter how pitiful I sounded when you first arrived. I haven't been just sitting around waiting to pounce on the first attractive female who happened to come my way, you know."

His wry tone made Josie abandon her dishrag and turn to face him. They were about three feet apart, with him leaning casually against the bar and her with her back to the counter near the sink. She was very, very conscious of that space between them, and she had the odd notion that he wanted to touch her and yet had made up his mind not to.

"We were talking about the ghost," she said.

"We've exhausted that subject for the time being," Marc said. "Now we're talking about us."

"There is no us. You're just bored, and—"

"Stop selling yourself short, Josie. This has nothing to do with me acting out of boredom—a thing I generally don't do, by the way. I'm also not in the habit of moving so fast when I find myself interested in a woman."

"Too fast," she blurted. "You're moving too fast."

"I know," he said unexpectedly. His smile was crooked. "I don't want to scare you off, believe me. I just . . . had to tell you that much at least. I

don't want you to think—as you obviously do—
that all I want is an amusing little flirtation to
while away the time until I go back to work. I admit I'm not thinking much beyond getting to
know you, but I definitely want to do that."

Very carefully, Josie said, "I came out here—
specifically looked for and picked a house in the
middle of nowhere—so that I could be alone to try
and write. Without interruptions or . . . distractions."

"You know what they say about the best-laid
plans," he murmured. Then he sighed and
shrugged a little. "In another two weeks, I'll be
back at work, and probably not even out here except on weekends. I'll try not to make a nuisance
of myself, really. That is—if you'll occasionally
take pity and spend a little time with me?"

Josie frowned suddenly. "You don't do humble
very well."

His wistful expression melted into amusement.
"Bear with me, it's a new emotion in my life."

She couldn't help but be a little amused, even
though she felt decidedly wary of him and definitely unsure of her own emotions about a possible
involvement with him. For nearly ten years all her
energy and attention had been focused on the task
she'd set for herself; she hadn't even considered
what she would do after it was all over, what direction her life might take.

What she did know for sure, what she had always known, was that she couldn't allow anything

—or anyone—to distract her or interfere with her plans. There was no room in her life right now for anything else. But she couldn't explain all that to Marc, and before she could frame the words to create some sort of delay to give herself time to think, he was speaking again in a matter-of-fact tone.

"There's no hurry, of course. You're still settling in here, and I won't be a hundred percent until after this cast comes off. We have plenty of time."

"Marc—"

"Plenty of time," he repeated. "Time to get to know each other, to talk. About the ghost of my ancestor, for instance, and why he's picked here and now for a visit. Which reminds me . . ." He stepped to the counter where Josie had left a pencil and notepad, and wrote something a bit awkwardly with his right hand. "The phone number at the cottage. In case old Luke decides to rattle a few chains in the middle of the night."

"Thanks," she murmured, deciding to accept the implicit offer neutrally.

"No, I should be saying that. Thanks for the shopping and the lunch."

"Don't mention it." Relieved that he was going, because she needed time alone to think about this, Josie followed him to the back door.

Halfway out, he paused and looked back past Josie at the cat sitting silently on one of the barstools. Almost hesitantly, he said, "Have you noticed anything . . . odd . . . about Pendragon? I mean—has he done anything especially *un*cat-like?"

Puzzled, Josie shook her head. "No, not that I've seen. He's been pretty catlike, on the whole."

"Oh." Marc smiled. "Of course. Well . . . thanks again. See you later."

Josie watched him across the garden, then shut the door and looked at Pendragon. "Now, what was that all about?"

Pendragon yawned and then began to purr. Loudly.

The remainder of the afternoon and evening passed uneventfully for Josie. She continued to settle in and get organized, familiarizing herself with the house and putting away her belongings so she could begin to feel at home. She found that she wasn't at all nervous, just as she'd told Marc, and even after darkness fell and the rain began coming down steadily, she found her surroundings more cozy than eerie.

She was not disturbed by another ghostly visitation, and Pendragon's key stayed where she'd rehung it on the hook by the cellar door. As for the black cat, he remained companionable and definitely catlike, doing nothing at all unusual except hiding his catnip mouse underneath her pillow and burrowing to find it in the middle of the night.

Friday dawned gray and wet. It continued to

rain steadily, discouraging any outdoor activities, and Josie was more than content to remain inside. She kept busy, reluctant to think too much about Marc and what he'd said, even though she couldn't seem to push him entirely out of her mind.

It was better not to think about him, she decided. Better to think about other things, even things she knew only too well would be painful.

She approached her task in the front parlor at last and spent most of the day in there getting organized. Her laptop computer was plugged in, its batteries charging; reference materials were unpacked and placed on the shelves of the secretary; and a stack of pristine legal pads as well as new boxes of sharpened pencils and the brand of pens she favored were on a table beside the comfortable sofa where she expected to do most of the work prior to the actual writing.

Josie put all the file boxes within reach of the sofa, wondering how long it would take her merely to organize all the information they contained into the most workable—and convincing—sequence of events. There was so much. Letters, notes, police reports and records, all the paperwork documenting investigations by arson experts and the insurance companies involved—and that was only part of it.

She didn't actually begin work, preferring to put that off at least another day, but Josie couldn't help sitting down just a minute and opening one file folder she was only too familiar with. Inside, yellowed and faded, its creases so worn they were practically disintegrating, was the entire front page of a major newspaper, dated twenty years before.

She didn't bother to unfold it. The picture and headline were enough. Even after so many years, after so much time spent staring at this, Josie felt the shock of it, the enormity of what had happened. The photo of a burning hotel was all too clear, the horror of helpless fireman and onlookers obvious.

The people jumping and falling to their deaths.

Two hundred and thirty people had died. *Two hundred and thirty people*.

As an accident, it would have been devastating. As arson, it was horrendous beyond belief. That anyone could have, in the dark quiet of a summer night, deliberately set fire to a hotel filled with people defied all understanding.

Then, it had shocked a nation. It was not, Josie reflected dismally, such a surprising thing today. Terrorism around the world had made such things more commonplace, had numbed the sense of disbelief that people could deliberately harm innocents for whatever reasons.

But even now, even after being numbed by terrorist bombs planted in shopping centers and restaurants and office buildings, even now the deliberate arson of a hotel for no other reason except the greedy desire for money still had the power to shock and enrage.

Even now a man who had deliberately or carelessly killed two hundred and thirty people by destroying heavily insured property was viewed as a monster.

Was a monster.

Josie unfolded the paper carefully and stared down at another picture on the front page. The black-and-white photo didn't show vibrant red hair or unusual violet eyes, but it did show a charming smile in a handsome face.

She didn't have to read the caption, because she'd read it so many times before. *Matthew Douglas is being questioned in the arson of his hotel.*

Josie touched the picture with the tips of her fingers and murmured, "I'll get him, Dad. I swear I'll get him."

FIVE

For once, the weather forecasters were right; the rain fell steadily and at times heavily all the way through Sunday night. Added to a chill breeze that often picked up energy and wailed mournfully, the rain hardly invited neighborly visits—even across a small but very wet garden.

Josie was relieved by that fact. Accustomed to being alone, she was rarely lonely, and if she thought from time to time of Marc, it was only— well, *mostly*—to remind herself that she didn't have the energy *or* the inclination to cope with charming lawyers no matter how much she might wish otherwise. She kept herself busy, talked to Pendragon, and generally kept her thoughts focused on why she was here and what she had to do.

The cat remained with her for the most part, but he did vanish for at least a couple of hours every day, returning with his glossy black fur wet, and suffering without protest or comment Josie drying him with a fluffy towel. She thought he probably visited Marc during those absences, and wondered idly why the cat had apparently adopted them both. It reminded her that she really should put an ad in the lost-and-found section of the local newspaper, and she made a mental note to herself to make the call on Monday.

And never mind that she hoped no one would claim Pendragon. He was far too personable a cat to be a stray, but although Josie felt guilty whenever she thought of someone—a child, perhaps, or lonely adult—yearning for their lost pet, she had the odd notion that Pendragon had decided where he should be, that he was no more lost than she was.

Still, she was duty bound to place the ad and had every intention of doing so. On Monday. Tuesday at the latest.

Sunday night brought a storm, which didn't disturb Josie until the lights flickered twice. Houses in the country, she reminded herself, did sometimes lose power because of lightning strikes or fallen trees, and it was best to be prepared for that eventuality. She had several flashlights, but she also remembered seeing a box of candles and at least two kerosene lamps in the cellar.

Accompanied by Pendragon, she went down to investigate. The lamps were where she'd remembered, both at least half-full of kerosene, and she carried them up to the kitchen triumphantly. She returned to the cellar to search for the box of candles, which proved far more elusive. Pendragon tried to help—from his point of view, anyway—but after Josie had to rescue him from a trunk she'd absentmindedly closed him in, she told him he'd be more help if he just sat down somewhere.

Offended, the big black cat stalked away, and a few minutes later Josie realized that he was sitting on a box and staring fixedly at Luke Westbrook's portrait.

She carried her small box of candles over to the cat and joined him in looking at the painting. "I think I would have liked him," she told the cat consideringly, able to study the roughly handsome face more objectively now that the memory of encountering his ghost had faded into dreamlike uncertainty.

"Yaaahh," Pendragon commented.

"I suppose I'd better cover him up again so he doesn't get dusty." She did so without bothering to check the other paintings stacked behind Luke's; since she didn't know enough about art to recognize a Rembrandt if she fell over one, Marc would have to find his own lost masterpiece, she decided.

With the portrait hidden once again, Pendragon looked down at the box he sat on and began to bat at a piece of tape that had come loose. Josie watched him momentarily, then frowned as she read the block-printed notation on the top and sides of the box. BOOKS.

"I have all mine in storage," she murmured, to the cat or to herself. "And if the weather in these parts stays as miserable as it's been so far, I'm going to be spending a lot of time indoors." She looked around briefly, realizing that this was the only box of books visible in the cellar.

Well, she doubted Marc would mind if she took the box upstairs and put the books on the now empty bookshelves in the den; books were always better off on shelves than packed away. And, besides, she might discover another kind of treasure for Marc if the books had been packed away long enough. A first edition, maybe, or perhaps copies of some of Luke Westbrook's own mysteries.

"Make way," she told Pendragon, gently nudging the cat off his seat. She set her small box of candles atop the medium-sized box of books, then lifted both of them carefully and took them upstairs. She put them in the den, where a cheerful fire burned and where she'd been watching a fuzzy picture on her small television set before going in search of emergency lighting.

The storm distracted her then, becoming rather violent, and she elected to turn off the TV before beginning a methodical search for the several candleholders she had seen in the house. It took about an hour to mate candles to holders and place them and matches about the house in strategic locations, but Josie felt better once it was done. One of the lamps, dusted and with wick trimmed, was placed in the den, while the other went to her bedroom.

She was coming back down the stairs when the power flickered again and the lights went completely out for three or four seconds—just long enough for Josie to catch a glimpse of something odd in the direction of the front parlor. When the lights came back on, she stood there on the bottom tread for a moment or two, indecisive.

The cat, probably. Except that what she'd seen looked like a kind of glow, and cats didn't glow. There was no fire in the parlor fireplace, and the light hadn't been a flash like lightning—just a kind of glow.

Finally she turned in the direction of the front parlor. She wouldn't be able to sleep tonight if she didn't check it out, she knew. Better to go and look, and satisfy herself that there was nothing weird.

Except that there was.

As Josie paused in the doorway, one hand lifted toward the light switch, a brilliant flash of lightning illuminated the room. And the man. He was standing near the fireplace, a frown on his harshly handsome face, looking around as if searching for something. And this time he didn't appear semi-transparent. This time he looked as real as any flesh-and-blood man would.

With perfectly eerie timing, the storm arrived overhead at that moment, massive with its own intensity. Thunder was a continuous roll of sense-numbing sound, and flashes of lightning came so swiftly that one dazzling burst of light followed another like a sequence of strobes.

Virtually blind between flashes, Josie could see only during them.

In that rapid series of stop-motion images, she saw the man turn his head and look toward the door, toward her. Still frowning, clearly frustrated now, he moved toward her. His left hand extended to her, imploring again, but this time with a touch of impatience.

Flash by flash, he was closer, seeming to glide rather than walk. His mouth was moving, but the thunder was so loud, it was all Josie could hear even if he was speaking, and ghosts couldn't speak, could they? Closer, his eyes so directly fixed on her face that she knew he saw her, she *knew* he did, and he wanted her to do something, he needed her to help him—

Her fumbling fingers touched the light switch at last, and a shaky breath left her as light flooded the room. Gone. Gone as if he'd never been there.

Josie leaned against the doorjamb, feeling her heart pounding against her ribs. Her knees felt weak, and she knew she was trembling. She wasn't frightened exactly—but definitely unnerved and shaken.

Would he have touched her if she hadn't turned on the light? Could he have? And why *had* he vanished when the light had been turned on? Before, in the hall upstairs, it had been shadowy;

here only lightning had illuminated him. Was there something about inorganic light that rendered a ghost invisible?

Now, *there* was a disturbing possibility. Maybe there were actually ghosts all around the living, everywhere and all the time, only they couldn't be seen in the unnatural light provided by electricity. . . .

Josie got a grip on herself. Nonsense. Of course it was nonsense. Because if they could only be seen in organic light, then why was sunlight apparently off-limits to them? Ghosts were always seen at night, everybody knew that, usually in the wee small hours after midnight. . . .

She looked at her watch and frowned, her intelligence beginning to take firm control of her nerves. Apparently, the ghost of Luke Westbrook had his own particular witching hour. It was just after ten, which was just about the same time of night she had seen him upstairs in the hallway. She had no idea why she hadn't seen him on any of the nights in between—unless it was simply because they hadn't been in the same room when he had made his nightly appearance?

Another disturbing thought.

Josie found herself backing away from the parlor door—and leaving the light on. She returned to the den, where Pendragon was curled up napping on the back of an overstuffed chair near the fireplace, and she just stood there for a few minutes almost compulsively stroking the cat and listening to the slowly diminishing sounds of the storm.

She was momentarily tempted to go into the kitchen and find the phone number Marc had left. It would have been nice to hear his deep voice, steady and reassuring . . . even if he didn't believe her. And this time he'd really be ready to have her hauled away and locked up. After all, what could she say to him?

Hey, guess what? Luke came calling again, but this time it was really creepy and I'd rather not be alone tonight. . . .

No. She wasn't going to ask him to run over and hold her hand, especially when he didn't believe her. She didn't need him. She refused to act like a frightened child when she was really only a little bit nervous. After all, Luke Westbrook hadn't done anything to her. Except send her blood pressure soaring to new heights, that is.

On the other hand, it seemed fairly obvious that he definitely wanted her to do something for him. And he was getting rather insistent about it.

It was only when she considered that point thoughtfully that Josie realized she had calmed down. Her pulse was normal, her knees no longer felt like jelly, and the urge to look nervously over her shoulder had faded. Good. Now she could try to figure out what Luke Westbrook expected her to do for him. . . .

Or she would in the morning. Right now it was

getting late, she was tired, and the storm was coming back. Or maybe it had never left.

Josie picked up the cat and went to bed.

"I know it was storming," Josie said with determined detachment. "And I know things always look and seem a little weird during storms. But I also know what I saw. And this time he looked as real as you do."

"But in the front parlor this time?" Marc asked.

"Yeah. He seemed to be looking for something. Then he saw me—and came toward me. I turned on the light just before he reached me, and he was gone."

"You still believe he wants something of you?"

"Definitely. In fact, I think he's getting impatient that I haven't already done whatever it is he wants me to do."

"From all I've heard and read," Marc said somewhat dryly, "that certainly sounds like Luke. He was well-known for his impatience."

They were on the porch, both of them half sitting on the sturdy railing and sipping coffee. It was midmorning, the temperature had risen to something approaching mild, and the sun was trying hard to push through gray clouds. Returning from his morning walk—slightly delayed by the weather —Marc had seen Josie on the porch and had come over.

"You weren't nervous after that?" he asked.

"Oddly enough, no. I thought I might be, but . . . I don't know. Even though last night was a little creepy, I'm not afraid of him." She tried to lighten her tone. "Of course, what I told you before stands—if he starts rattling chains, I'm out of here."

"I can't say I'd blame you."

Josie smiled suddenly. "Your friend didn't happen to tell you how to exorcise ghosts, did he?"

It took Marc a moment to remember that he'd mentioned Tucker's brief fascination with the paranormal. "No, I gather that wasn't his aim. He wanted to meet one—in the flesh, so to speak."

Dryly, Josie said, "Then you might want to invite him out here one night. As far as I can tell, the show starts just after ten."

Marc frowned and spoke slowly. "Just after ten every night? You didn't tell me—"

"Well, I haven't seen him every night. Although it *did* occur to me that maybe we just weren't in the same room when he decided to appear. But both times I have seen him, it was a little after ten o'clock. Why? Is that significant?"

He hesitated, then said, "According to the police report, Luke died between ten and midnight."

"Oh." A useful syllable, Josie thought vaguely. Indicating a variety of possible responses. Acknowledgment. Comprehension. Oh, I see. Oh, I understand. And it filled the silence nicely when one just didn't know *what* to say.

Then she did know what to say. "Wait a minute, now. He died fifty years ago, and you know what the police report says? What is it, family folklore?"

Marc shook his head. "As a matter of fact, I . . . found a biography of Luke among some of the books in the cottage, and I've been reading up on his life. And death. It was written by somebody who'd known him and published a little more than a year after he died."

"I'd like to borrow it when you've finished," Josie said.

"Sure." In a rather careful tone, Marc said, "Look, if my ancestor is lurking about the place, I'd sort of like to see him. Do you suppose I could come over tonight? Say, a little before ten? We could always roast marshmallows, or pop popcorn. And I can bring the bio; I should be finished with it."

"What if he doesn't appear tonight?"

"Nothing ventured. And there's always tomorrow."

Having more or less decided to do everything in her power to discourage Marc from spending time with her, Josie should have either come up with some excuse or simply refused outright. That was what she should have done. What she planned to do.

But that wasn't what came out of her mouth.

"Sure, why not. I'll even supply the popcorn and marshmallows."

"Terrific." Marc handed over his empty cup. "Thanks for the coffee. I'm going to go away now and let you get to work."

"Work?"

"Your writing. Remember?"

Josie felt her face getting hot. "Oh, right. Luke's visit sort of pushed everything else out of my head."

"Understandable." Marc's voice was grave.

She had a feeling he knew very well that it hadn't been Luke but his descendant who had pushed work out of her mind. She found herself looking at him and feeling peculiarly exposed for an instant, almost frighteningly vulnerable, as if something, some curtain, that had been hanging between them was suddenly stripped away.

There was too much of him. It wasn't just that he was tall and powerful and so impressively hand-some; it wasn't only the intelligence and humor in his tarnished-silver eyes or the charm of his smile; it wasn't even the deep and beautifully liquid voice that surely must have swayed more than one jury. No, what overwhelmed her most of all was some-thing far more elusive in him, something she could only sense.

He was . . .

Whatever he was, whatever she felt about him was thrust away violently as Josie looked away from him. She wondered if she was breathing, and her voice sounded shockingly normal when she said, "See you tonight, then."

Marc didn't appear to notice anything peculiar, or at least didn't comment if he did. He merely said, "I'll be here," and then headed back toward the cottage.

Far more unnerved than she had been by the appearance of a ghost, she nevertheless couldn't help watching him as he crossed the garden. Maybe that was the worst of it. That she couldn't fight the urge to watch him.

If she hadn't known he had injured his leg, she wouldn't have suspected anything; his stride was steady and even, she thought absently. And convalescence certainly hadn't robbed him of his athletic build, that was for sure. He was definitely a man people—especially women—would always notice. Powerful shoulders, a narrow waist, obvious strength. Despite forced inactivity, he still looked as if he was physically capable of doing just about anything he wanted to do. . . .

Josie felt her face get hot as, totally unbidden, sensual images filled her mind. It was something that she could not remember ever happening to her before, and she was even more unsettled when pushing them out of her head proved difficult. Very difficult.

Pendragon jumped up onto the railing just then, balancing easily, and sat down to regard her with feline inscrutability.

"What's wrong with me?" she demanded of the cat with more than a trace of panic.

For once, however, the very responsive Pendragon had nothing to say. He just sat there, tail curled neatly around forepaws, and looked at her. And surely it was her imagination that his permanent cat-smile curled at the corners even more than usual and his china-blue eyes gleamed with an almost human amusement.

Surely.

By the time Marc came over at slightly before nine-thirty that evening, Josie had all her walls up. She'd spent most of the day in the front parlor working, and between that grim task—so far, she hadn't been able to summon any kind of detachment—and her uneasy awareness of her growing attraction to Marc, she was feeling decidedly upset.

"Here's the book," he said cheerfully when she let him in.

"Thanks, I'll get it back to you as soon as I've read it." Josie led the way into the den, where a brisk fire and a number of lamps provided a warm and cozy atmosphere.

"There's no hurry. Hello, cat." He paused at the overstuffed chair to stroke Pendragon briefly and looked around the room with an appreciative gaze. "This is nice."

Josie didn't ask whether he meant the general ambience of a crackling fire on a chilly evening or the very few things—some needlepoint pillows, scattered knickknacks, and two casual arrangements of colorful fall foliage in vases—she had used to give the room a more personal feel.

"Have a seat," she invited, setting the book he'd brought her on the wooden coffee table. "I've made some spice tea; I thought it would go well with popcorn or marshmallows. Would you like some?"

"Please." Marc watched her retreat to the kitchen, then frowned down at Pendragon and muttered, "She all but called me Mr. Westbrook."

"Yaaa-woo," the cat commented, just as softly.

Marc sensed commiseration and scratched behind the cat's ear fleetingly before going to sit on the couch. She wasn't freezing him out, he thought, but Josie had definitely withdrawn behind walls of polite blandness.

It was baffling. She was baffling. She seemed determined to keep him guessing. Or something. This morning she had been a bit wary, but only— he'd thought—because she'd been describing another ghostly visitation and was apprehensive of disbelief. And just before he'd left her on the porch, he would have *sworn* there had been something else. A surprising moment when he'd been sure she had really looked at him, had seen him— maybe for the first time.

And now all these walls. So . . . either she hadn't liked what she'd seen, or something else had driven her to hide from him. Which presented him with something of a choice. He could pretend her manner was completely normal and just wait to see what would happen next, or else he could ask what the hell was wrong.

Logic told him the former would be preferable if he didn't want Josie to feel pressed in any way, but a miserably wet weekend spent alone in the cottage with only brief visits from Pendragon had inexorably worn away his patience. Why shouldn't he ask what was wrong? Something obviously was. And he of all people should certainly know that you couldn't find answers if you didn't ask questions.

Josie came back into the den, offering him a mug of steaming spice tea and a smile so impersonal he might have been the man who'd just put gas in her car. She took her own mug and sat down in the overstuffed chair with the black cat curled up behind her bright red head.

Marc tried to be charitable. Perhaps that was just her favorite chair—and never mind that less than a week in a place was arguably not enough time to develop such habits. Maybe she just liked sitting near the cat. Or maybe it was something else.

He sipped his tea, nodding enjoyment of the tangy blend of cinnamon, orange, and other spices. Then, looking steadily at Josie, he spoke in a reflective voice, like a man ticking off important points on his fingers.

"I am an officer of the court. I've practiced law in Richmond for some time now, and any number of intelligent, respectable people would probably be willing to vouch for my character. My doctor has known me since college—and he knows me inside out even in the most literal sense—so he could certainly allay any doubts you might have as to my general health, physical and mental. I'd be glad to furnish my sister's phone number; sisters are brutally honest, you know, unlike mothers who do tend to be biased. I imagine I could even get my school transcripts—"

"Marc, what are you talking about?"

He gave her his best guileless expression. "Wasn't I being clear? Sorry. It's just that you obviously view me as a potential ax murderer or, at the very least, a threat to your virtue, and I thought I might need to produce character references."

"I never suggested you were anything like that," she said uncomfortably, the wall beginning to crack.

"You didn't have to say a word." Deliberately, he allowed his gaze to examine the three quarters of the couch stretching out emptily beside him. When he looked at Josie again, the walls were definitely coming down; a delicate color had spread over her cheeks, and her dismay was obvious.

She'd never be able to hide embarrassment, self-consciousness, or anger even behind her walls, he thought, watching her. Nature had made that impossible by stamping a strong blush response into her genes. He liked it—not because it made her feelings so obvious, but because the extra color in her face turned her eyes the most incredible shade of pale violet. . . .

He got a grip on himself and kept his voice gently reflective. "If you'd prefer a more detached opinion, I'm sure the president of my bank would—"

"Stop it." She didn't quite snap the words, but almost. And she wasn't hiding at all now, behind walls or anything else. Those lovely, fierce eyes regarded him with resentment and annoyance and no little indignation.

Marc had spent too much time learning to read witnesses not to know that most of her emotions stemmed from sheer embarrassment, so he didn't hesitate to keep gently hammering away.

"I'm sure you're right to discount my attempts to prove I'm perfectly safe. Family and friends, even business associates, can hardly be counted upon to provide accurate testimony about a man's character. Why, even the most malevolent serial killer can produce dozens of shocked neighbors and relatives to exclaim, 'But he seemed so normal!' "

Glaring now, Josie said, "Now, *there's* a reassuring thought."

"Isn't it? And it leaves me in the painful position of not knowing how to convince you I can be trusted. You obviously don't believe me. In fact, I have the impression that even if I had a visible halo, it wouldn't cut any ice with you."

Josie gnashed her teeth almost audibly, but

then frowned in a new way. "Why am I letting you put me on the defensive? Dammit, I haven't known you a week."

In an interested tone, he asked, "Do you have a set amount of time that must pass before you decide it isn't necessary to sit on the other side of the room? Or is it a matter of territory? At the cottage, you sat beside me; are things different on your own turf? I'm only asking because a man likes to know these things."

"You're asking because it amuses you to make fun of me." This time she did snap.

Marc shook his head. "Now, you see? There you go thinking the worst of me again. When all I was trying to do was to narrow this chasm you've put between us."

"Chasm? It looks like a coffee table to me."

"It's the Grand Canyon."

"Stop exaggerating. It's about six feet."

Rueful, he said, "And lawyers get accused of having literal minds."

For the first time tonight Josie smiled a real smile. Not as if she wanted to, but Marc was encouraged. "Why don't we compromise, and meet each other halfway? That's a nice, thick hearth rug, with plenty of room between the coffee table and the fireplace for us to sit. We need to be closer anyway. To roast the marshmallows."

He waited, patient and intent, watching her hesitation, seeing the swift play of emotions across her delicate face. With her walls down, the feelings were startlingly naked, stealing his breath with their honesty.

Fading irritation. Uncertainty. Anxiety and longing. Wariness. The fleeting ache of some deep pain. And, finally, a fragile dignity.

She leaned forward and put her mug on the coffee table, then rose and turned to the kitchen. "I'll get the popcorn and marshmallows," she murmured.

Marc had all but forgotten he had ostensibly come over here to catch a glimpse of his long-dead ancestor. He wasn't much interested in ghosts at the moment. He was fully and completely interested in Josie.

Deciding to assume her acceptance of his suggestion, he left the couch and moved around the coffee table. The hearth rug was comfortably thick, and a couple of her pillows made leaning back against the coffee table satisfactory. Absently, he picked up the poker and reached to stir the fire, causing the flames to leap higher.

Did she know how nakedly emotions showed on her face with the walls gone? She had to know. *Maybe that's where the walls came from. Maybe someone saw what she felt, and used it to hurt her.*

From the first day they had met, Marc had been aware of her guardedness, but he had supposed it was only the ordinary caution between strangers. Now he was convinced she had built a wall for herself out of necessity. Without that barrier, Josie was so vulnerable it was almost terrifying.

She would raise it again, of course, if not tonight then tomorrow. Self-preservation would demand it of her. But now that he had seen inside, she wouldn't be able to shut him out as she had done. Now he knew the way in.

When Josie came back into the den, she joined him on the hearth rug without hesitation or comment—with a careful foot of space between them. She had a bag of marshmallows and two long, thin metal skewers obviously designed for roasting marshmallows or shish kebabs. And she had a long-handled metal basket.

"Did you know this stuff was here?" she asked him. "The skewers and the corn popper?"

"I wasn't sure, but I knew we'd done this sort of thing as kids here. Where did you find them?"

"In one of the lower cabinets in the kitchen." She twisted around to put the skewers and marshmallows on the coffee table, then checked the corn popper. "I've never used one of these before."

"Let me," Marc said.

She handed it over willingly and watched as he leaned forward and held the popper close to the crackling fire. After a few quiet minutes the corn began to pop—at first slowly and then with more enthusiasm. It wasn't long before they were munching on popcorn from the basket set on the rug between them.

"Very good," she offered.

"Thank you. It's all in the wrist."

"I'll remember that." She hesitated, then commented neutrally, "It's nearly ten."

Marc didn't respond for a moment, then asked, "Do we search the house for him, or let him come to us?"

Josie glanced at him and shrugged. "Both times I saw him, I was basically just minding my own business. Searching the house probably doesn't make sense."

"Then we wait." Marc turned a bit more to face her, resting his left arm on the coffee table. "Still mad at me?"

"For what?" She didn't look at him.

Even with only her profile available, he could see her tension, see her vulnerability. "For needling you," he replied, completely serious.

"Is that what you were doing?"

"More or less. I could have just demanded to know why the hell you couldn't sit beside me, but I had a suspicion that wouldn't have gotten me anywhere at all."

"And needling did?"

"You want me to tell you what you're feeling right now?"

She almost flinched away from that, as if he'd struck her or threatened to, and stared fixedly into the fire with color burning in her face.

Marc wanted to touch her, to somehow reassure her that he wouldn't hurt her, but he was even more determined to hold on to this moment long enough to understand her. "Josie, why do you have to push me away? Why can't you let me get close to you?" He kept his voice quiet.

"Hasn't it occurred to you that I'm just not interested?" She obviously tried hard to sound cold, but her voice quavered.

"No," he replied. "Because I know that isn't the answer. I knew the night I kissed you. I'm not a kid, Josie. I know when a woman wants me."

Still without looking at him, she said tightly, "Do you notch your bedpost?"

He shook his head. "Don't try to convince yourself that I'm just out for what I can get. I'm not into one-night stands *or* brief affairs—if I were, do you really think I would have kept my hands to myself all this time?"

"How do I know?"

"You know. For God's sake, trust your instincts. I'm no plaster saint, but I'm not a monster either, you must know that. I've never knowingly hurt anyone in my life, and the last thing I want to do is hurt you."

"That's not—" She broke off abruptly.

"That's not what you're worried about? Then, what, Josie? If it isn't me?"

She turned her head finally and looked at him, only a little color in her cheeks now and her glorious eyes darkened. "It's me." Her voice was soft, almost inaudible. "There's no . . . no room in me, don't you understand?"

He matched her grave tone. "No, I don't understand."

She shook her head helplessly. "There's no room. I have all I can handle, more than I can handle sometimes—" She steadied her voice. "I can't take anything else in my life. Not now. I came out here to—to simplify everything, not to make it even more complicated."

"I'm a complication?"

"Yes."

"Why? Because I want you?"

Color came and went rapidly in her cheeks. "Marc . . . haven't you ever been . . . consumed by something going on in your life? A case that was incredibly difficult or—or something in your personal life that took all your energy to resolve?"

"A few times," he said slowly. "Cases that seem to demand every waking moment."

She nodded slightly. "It's like that. My—my writing. I've given myself a year, and I worked very hard to make that possible. Now I have to focus, to concentrate. I can't afford any distractions."

"You can't write twenty-four hours a day."

"You know that isn't what I mean."

It was his turn to nod, but what he said was, "That friend of mine—the one who got interested in the paranormal—is also a rather well-known writer. He tells me that some writers make the mistake of believing they have to isolate them-

Get swept away...

Enter the

Winner's Classic Sweepstakes

and discover that love has its own rewards.

You could win a romantic 14-day rendezvous for two in diamond-blue Hawaii...the gothic splendor of Europe...or the sun-drenched Caribbean. To enter, make your choice with one of these tickets. If you win, you'll be swept away to your destination *with $5,000 cash!*

Get 4 FREE Loveswept Romances!

or take $25,000 Cash!

Whisk me to Hawaii

Carry Me Off To Europe

Take me to the Caribbean

Pamper me with FREE GIFTS!

GET A FREE GIFT!

Get this personal, lighted makeup case. It's yours absolutely FREE!

NO OBLIGATION TO BUY.
See details inside...

Get Swept Away To Your Romantic Holiday!

Imagine being wrapped in the embrace of your lover's arms, watching glorious Hawaiian rainbows born only for you. Imagine strolling through the gothic haunts of romantic London. Imagine being drenched in the sun-soaked beauty of the Caribbean. If you crave such journeys then enter now to...

WIN YOUR ROMANTIC RENDEZVOUS PLUS $5,000 CASH!
Or Take $25,000 CASH!

Seize the moment and enter to win one of these exotic 14-day rendezvous for two, plus $5,000.00 CASH! To enter affix the destination ticket of your choice to the Official Entry Form and drop it in the mail. It costs you absolutely nothing to enter—not even postage! So take a chance on romance and enter today!

Has More In Store For You With 4 FREE BOOKS and a FREE GIFT!

We've got four FREE Loveswept Romances and a FREE Lighted Makeup Case ready to send you!

Place the FREE GIFTS ticket on your Entry Form, and your first shipment of Loveswept Romances is yours absolutely FREE—*and that means no shipping and handling.*

Plus, about once a month, you'll get four *new* books hot off the presses, *before they're in the bookstores.* You'll always have 15 days to decide whether to keep any shipment, for our low regular price, currently just $11.95.* **You are never obligated to keep any shipment**, and you may cancel at any time by writing "cancel" across our invoice and returning the shipment to us, at our expense. There's **no risk** and **no obligation** to buy, *ever.*

It's a pretty seductive offer, we've made even more attractive with the **Lighted Makeup Case—yours absolutely FREE!** It has an elegant tortoise-shell finish, an assortment of brushes for eye shadow, blush and lip color. And with the lighted makeup mirror *you* can make sure he'll always see the passion in your eyes!

BOTH GIFTS ARE ABSOLUTELY FREE AND ARE YOURS TO KEEP FOREVER, no matter what you decide about future shipments! So come on! You risk nothing at all—and you stand to gain a world of sizzling romance, exciting prizes...and FREE GIFTS!

*(plus shipping & handling, and sales tax in NY and Canada)

ENTER NOW TO WIN A ROMANTIC RENDEZVOUS FOR TWO

Plus $5,000 CASH!

or take $25,000 Cash!

No risk and no obligation to buy, anything, *ever!*

Winners Classic

SWEEPSTAKES
OFFICIAL ENTRY FORM

☐ **YES!** Enter me in the sweepstakes! I've affixed the destination ticket for the Romantic Rendezvous of my choice to this Entry Form. I've also affixed the FREE GIFTS ticket. So please, send me my 4 FREE BOOKS and FREE Lighted Makeup Case.

DETACH CAREFULLY AND MAIL TODAY

Affix Destination Ticket of Your Choice Here	TICKET	Affix FREE GIFTS Ticket Here	🎁

PLEASE PRINT CLEARLY   CK1   12237

NAME

ADDRESS

CITY   APT. #

STATE   ZIP

There is no purchase necessary to enter the sweepstakes. To enter without taking advantage of the risk-free offer, return the entry form with only the romantic rendezvous ticket affixed. To be eligible, sweepstakes entries must be received by the deadline found in the accompanying rules at the back of the book. There is no obligation to buy when you send for your free books and free lighted makeup case. You may preview each new shipment for 15 days free. If you decide against it, simply return the shipment within 15 days and owe nothing. If you keep them, pay our low regular price, currently just $2.99 each book —a savings of $.50 per book off the cover price (plus shipping & handling, and sales tax in NY and Canada.)

Prices subject to change. Orders subject to approval. See complete sweepstakes rules at the back of the book.

Don't miss your chance to win a romantic rendezvous for two and get 4 FREE BOOKS and a FREE Lighted Makeup Case!

You risk nothing—so enter now!

selves in order to hear their muse. But it doesn't work that way. A writer has to be like a sponge, soaking up information and experiences."

"Maybe some writers—"

"Josie, if you can't tell me the truth, then just say it's none of my business. Tell me to go to hell or otherwise get lost. But don't lie to me." He knew his voice had roughened, but he couldn't seem to do anything about it.

Her eyes widened. "Lie? I'm not—"

"Yes, you are. I think you are *consumed* by something, but it isn't writing. There's no joy in you when you talk about it. No excitement or uncertainty. No frustration or anxiety. Just . . . resolution. And that's all wrong. If you were a writer who'd reached the point of taking a year to find out if you were any good, your whole attitude would be different.

"But if you aren't a writer—then what are you? What *did* you take a year off to do? What is it that takes up so much of your energy and yourself that you have . . . no room left?"

SIX

For a moment, gazing into tarnished-silver eyes that saw too much, Josie was tempted to tell him the truth. But it had become a conditioned reflex to shy away, to avoid talking about what had happened to her father. Definitely once and probably twice in the past twenty years, confiding had cost her a romance, and it had definitely cost her at least one friend.

She had learned to be wary.

Slowly, carefully, because she had a notion something would break if she wasn't cautious, she said, "I don't think Luke is going to show up tonight. Perhaps you should go."

A muscle flexed in his jaw. "Perhaps I should. But I'd like you to answer something—honestly—before I go."

She didn't say she'd have to hear it first; both of them knew that. So she merely waited.

"Are you so sure there's no room in your life for me? So sure that you aren't even willing to give us a chance?"

"I'm sure." But she wasn't, and even she could hear that in her voice. Already, he'd gotten too close, and she didn't even know how he'd done it.

"Are you?" Without another word, Marc leaned over and covered her startled lips with his in an abrupt kiss.

He didn't hold her in place; his unencumbered right hand lifted, but only to lie gently against her neck while his thumb brushed her jaw. Yet she couldn't escape him.

She didn't want to escape him.

If the first kiss between them, days ago, had shaken her, this one was devastating. It was as if her body, stirred awake by his touch, recognized him as its master in some deeply primitive way she hardly understood. All she knew was that she could no more prevent her response than she could willfully stop the beating of her heart.

There was nothing tentative about Marc, nothing hesitant. He wanted her, and he meant her to have no doubts about that. His mouth plundered hers, not bruising and yet with a hungry intensity that flooded her senses with molten heat. She was hardly aware of turning more toward him until her thigh pushed against the corn popper between them and her hands touched his chest.

The flannel of his shirt was soft beneath her fingers, and beneath the shirt his body was surprisingly hard, with little give to the flesh. He smelled of a spicy musk and woodsmoke, the combination curiously potent. Josie heard a faint sound escape her, shockingly sensual, and his heart was pounding beneath her hand, or maybe it was her own pulse she felt. . . .

The hardness of his cast brushed past her shoulder, and his fingers touched her hair near her temple. His right hand still lay against her neck, those fingers brushing her nape in a whisper touch she found wildly arousing, and his mouth was moving on hers, his tongue a shattering possession.

She wanted, suddenly and violently, to be closer to him, to feel the powerful length of his body against hers. She wanted their clothing gone, wanted them naked together here in front of the fire. She wanted to feel his hands on her bare skin, and his lips, and she wanted to touch him with a longing so vast and overpowering it was dimly terrifying.

Dazed, she opened her eyes to stare at him when he drew away abruptly. Her fingers were clutching his shirt, she realized, holding on as if to a lifeline.

"*Are* you sure, Josie?" he demanded, his normally liquid voice a hoarse rasp. "Are you sure now?"

He was really the most incredibly handsome man she'd ever seen. Dramatically handsome.

Striking. And sexy, God knew. And those eyes . . .

Then his demanding question sank in, and she blinked in confusion. "What?" she managed, making a vain effort to slow her breathing.

"Are you sure there's no room in your life for me?" Without waiting for an answer, he kissed her again, briefly and a bit roughly this time, and his silvery eyes gleamed at her.

"No," she whispered.

His jaw tightened. "No, you aren't sure? Or—"

She forced herself to let go of his shirt and ordered her shaking hands to lie on her thighs. She felt color rush to her face and hoped desperately that he couldn't read her feelings this time. She didn't want him to realize that she hadn't been answering his question at all, that she had been protesting something else entirely.

No, don't stop. Please don't stop. . . .

"Josie—"

"No, I—I'm not sure of anything anymore." Her voice was husky, almost a whisper.

The hardness in his expression softened and he kissed her again, quickly and lightly. "Don't sound so lost," he murmured, stroking her hot cheek gently.

She felt lost. And she felt . . . unfamiliar to herself. Where was her certainty, her resolve to allow nothing to distract her from her plans? For so long, for nearly ten years, everything in her had been so focused, and now . . . now she could hardly think at all. God, what had the man done to her?

"I have to think," she murmured.

Marc seemed to hesitate, then said softly, "You want me. Admit it, Josie."

"No, I—"

"Admit it."

She couldn't look away from him. And, no matter how much she wanted to resist saying it, because putting it into words made it too real to be denied, she heard herself telling him what he wanted to hear. Telling him the truth.

"I—I want you."

He nodded slowly, satisfaction gleaming in his eyes. "And you know I want you, don't you?"

The heat of his desire was so indelibly stamped into her consciousness—perhaps even her very skin—that she could only nod a bit helplessly. He was still stroking her cheek with just the tips of his fingers, and she had to fight the urge to lean into the caress, to press herself against him. She wanted him to kiss her again, and she was painfully aware that her longing was as plain as neon to him.

He began to lean toward her, but then stopped himself with obvious effort and slowly took his hands off her. "If I don't leave right now," he told her huskily as he rose to his feet, "I won't leave at all. As much as I want to stay, I don't think you're ready to take me to your bed."

Josie turned her gaze to the fire as quickly as she could, hoping he couldn't see the disappointment she felt. *Oh, God, what has he done to me?* She didn't get up because she was quite sure her legs wouldn't support her, and even if he *could* read her emotions, she wasn't going to confirm what the man already knew by collapsing at his feet.

"Josie?"

"Good night, Marc." Her voice held steady, rather to her surprise.

"Good night." He hesitated for a moment, and she thought she felt him touch her hair fleetingly, and then he left.

She sat there for a long time, her eyes fixed blindly on the fire, then sighed and stirred. She really should get up. Take the leftover popcorn and unused marshmallows to the kitchen. Bank the fire for the night. And then go upstairs. Maybe soaking in a hot tub would ease the tension from her muscles.

But she doubted it.

Still not trusting her legs, she twisted around to use the coffee table as leverage—and then froze, both hands planted firmly. She blinked, carefully. Stared while her sluggish mind grappled with an impossibility.

Lying on top of the biography of Luke Westbrook that Marc had brought in tonight was a small brass key, its loop of ribbon faded. It lay there innocently, winking in the firelight. Just a key. Except that it shouldn't have been there. Josie was sure it *hadn't* been there when she had joined Marc on the hearth rug, because she would have noticed the pale gleam against the darkness of the book's cover.

No, it had been hanging in the kitchen, on the cup hook by the cellar door. Where she had left it.

She looked quickly at Pendragon, only to find the cat still curled up, eyes closed, with all the appearance of a cat who hadn't moved in hours. Which wasn't to say that he *hadn't* moved in hours. He could have, she supposed. He could have leaped up high enough to somehow get the key. And then he could have brought it in here and left it on the book.

But why on earth would he have done that?

After a moment she reached across the coffee table and picked up the key. She stared at it, fingers probing, searching out solidity, reality.

Yes, it was real.

Right. And, assuming the cat hadn't fetched it, it had floated in from the kitchen sometime during the last hour or so, landing on Luke's bio. . . .

Hardly aware of speaking aloud, Josie murmured, to herself and to the cat, "An odd place to land no matter which of you did it. Coincidence is a fine thing, but I think Luke's trying to tell me something."

Well, what the hell. She was reasonably sure she wouldn't sleep a wink tonight anyway, considering the frustration aching in every muscle and tingling in every nerve. And she'd drive herself crazy if she spent the night agonizing about Marc. So why not just take the book to bed and read about Luke Westbrook?

With any luck at all, she'd figure out what, if anything, one small brass key had to do with a long-dead mystery writer. And why he was haunting her.

With any luck at all . . .

It was chilly outside, but Marc didn't hurry as he walked through the moonlight back to the cottage. Neither the cold air nor the exercise had any effect on his frustration. He hadn't really expected it to. It had taken every ounce of willpower and determination he'd been able to summon to get up and leave Josie, especially after she had looked at him with that heart-stopping yearning in her lovely face.

He was a masochist. It was a hell of a thing to discover about himself after thirty-five relatively blameless years, but he couldn't ignore the evidence. Any sane man who could walk away from Josie when he knew—*he knew*—he could have spent the night in bed with her making love had to be a masochist.

There was just no other word for it.

If someone had put him on the witness stand and invited him to explain himself and his ridiculous scruples, he wasn't sure he'd have been able to. What, after all, could he say? That he wanted more? That he wanted her to want him with the same unshadowed intensity with which he wanted her?

Dammit, I want to make sure she doesn't have the slightest inclination to kick me out of her bed and out of her life the morning after!

And that was it, really. He could make Josie want him, make her forget all the doubts and reservations and outright resistance to the mere idea of involvement with him—but he had seen all those things in her remarkable eyes before desire had clouded them, and he couldn't forget it.

The simple truth was that Josie wouldn't choose, eyes wide open in the cool light of day, to be his lover. Not now. Not yet. And until she made that choice . . .

He stirred the dying fire in his fireplace and piled on fresh wood, then sat on the couch and broodingly watched the flames. When the phone rang, he jumped only slightly and was able to reassure Tucker that, no, he hadn't been asleep.

"In fact," he told his friend wryly, "I've never been farther from sleep."

"Dare I hazard a guess?"

"You will, no matter what I say."

"True. In my experience, only two kinds of troubles keep a man from his just sleep. Love or money. And I know you don't need money."

Marc stared at the crackling fire until it blurred a bit. He was suddenly aware of his heart beating, slow and heavy, aching in his chest. Another definition of a masochist, he thought dimly, would probably be a man in love with a wary woman he'd met barely a week before.

"No," he said finally. "No, I don't need money."

Instead of crowing in triumph or otherwise giving Marc a hard time, Tucker offered a sober, "If we're talking about Josie Douglas, then I have a hunch you've got your work cut out for you, my friend."

"Why?"

"Because as near as I can figure, the lady has been through several kinds of hell in the last twenty years. It might be my writer's imagination, of course, but if she's a sensitive soul, I doubt she finds it easy to let anybody get close to her."

"You've finished the background search? So quickly?"

Still grave, Tucker said, "Something neither of us expected. She's not anonymous, Marc. Up until ten years ago, when her father died and she went to the other side of the country to attend college, there was quite a bit written about her in national and West Coast newspapers. And in tabloids."

Marc drew a breath. "Start at the beginning, Tucker."

"It was more like an ending. The ending of a

normal life." Tucker sighed. "Seattle. Twenty years ago this past summer, in 1974. A hotel belonging to Matthew Douglas—Josie's father—was deliberately set on fire. It was late at night and . . . well, two hundred and thirty people died. The hotel was heavily insured, and Douglas was rumored to be on the verge of bankruptcy. He was eventually arrested and charged."

"My God." Marc felt grim. "Matthew Douglas."

"We would have been about fifteen," Tucker observed. "I don't remember the trial. Girls, football, and Watergate had my attention. How about you?"

"The same. But one of my professors in law school liked to review sensational court cases. That was one of them."

"Remember the details?"

"It's been a while. Fill me in, will you? And tell me everything you've found out about Josie."

She fell asleep around four A.M., having finished the biography of Luke Westbrook and having spent half an hour after reading it staring at the ceiling above her bed.

Luke's bed.

Her dreams were unsettled, which was hardly surprising. Keys were everywhere, hung by faded loops of ribbon from doorknobs and light switches. And then there were the men. If it wasn't a handsome lawyer trying to kiss her in every dark corner of the house, it was a handsome ghost beckoning urgently—and all the time an enigmatic black cat kept appearing suddenly wherever she happened to be and grinning at her like a cross between the Grinch and the Cheshire cat.

By nine Josie was up and in the shower, trying to wash away the gritty-eyed feeling of fatigue that came from too little sleep and too many problems chasing their own tails. She was drinking coffee and eating toast in the kitchen when the crunch of gravel alerted her to the arrival of a visitor, but by the time she made it to a front window, all she saw was a rather nice Jeep Cherokee parked near her van.

After an anxious moment she realized it must be one of Marc's friends, and when she returned to the kitchen and looked out the back window, she saw a tall, casually dressed blond man passing through the garden toward the cottage. She thought, but wasn't sure, that he carried a little black bag.

The doctor friend? It seemed likely.

Josie would have liked to meet him, but she was a long way from being ready to face Marc. The vulnerability of last night was still very much with her, and she was no closer to understanding how he could have such an overwhelming effect on her.

There was a large part of her that shied away

from even considering the matter, a part that reminded her she had a task to complete and couldn't allow any distraction—even a devastating lawyer or an insistent ghost—to sidetrack her.

Which was all very well and good, but an hour or so later, as she attempted to work in the front parlor, Josie discovered that she had filled a page of a legal pad with doodles of keys, quill pens, and —most surprisingly of all—a rather good sketch of a handsome, dramatic face with a widow's peak and light, striking eyes.

"This is absurd," she told Pendragon, who was sitting companionably at the other end of the couch. "Three men fighting for my attention, and two of them are dead."

"Yaaa-woo," the cat said softly.

Sensing commiseration, Josie smiled at him. "Thanks, pal. But something a little more constructive would be nice. Like a suggestion."

Apparently, all Pendragon could offer was sympathy, since he began washing a forepaw methodically.

Josie sighed and studied the legal pad. She certainly didn't need an expert to tell her that her mind was indeed filled with turmoil. She also didn't need that same expert to point out that, given a choice between the grim task of reliving her father's tragedy and exploring the mystery of Luke and her growing fascination with Marc, Josie was naturally leaning toward the Westbrook men.

Even if Marc left her confused and unsure of herself, there was also more than a thread of exhilaration and the inescapable temptation to experience a kind of passion unlike anything she had ever felt before.

As for Luke, the puzzle of what he required of her was intriguing enough even without the eeriness of his being a ghost, and she *did* want to get that situation resolved.

"It's very simple, really," she told Pendragon, this time in a tone of relief. "The short-term problems should be dealt with first. That means Luke. At least, I hope he's short-term. Anyway, he's obviously not going to leave me in peace until I do whatever it is he wants me to do. Right?"

"Yah," the cat replied.

Josie eyed him suspiciously.

Pendragon blinked, then said, "Mmaaaarrc?"

After a startled moment Josie said, "Cats *never* use *k* sounds or hard *c*'s. Never."

"Mmaaaarrc," Pendragon repeated, quite distinctly, almost coughing the difficult hard *c*.

Josie decided that she had spent entirely too much time talking to the cat. Because she was sure he had said "Marc," and that was, naturally, ridiculous. Even so, she heard herself ask uneasily, "What about him?"

"Prruptt," Pendragon replied, lapsing back into cat.

She was about to ask him to clarify that, when

he started suddenly and jumped down from the couch, hurrying from the room as if he had abruptly remembered an appointment.

Josie shook her head bemusedly as she gazed after him, then looked back at the legal pad. Well. The logic definitely made sense. She would temporarily postpone the work of putting together the case to vindicate her father; she had a year, after all. And she would concentrate on solving the mystery of Luke Westbrook.

What about Marc?

Her mind wanted to shy away, but she held it firmly as though it were a skittish horse. Marc. She thought Marc would be every bit as insistent as his ancestor; it seemed to run in the family. He wanted her, and he'd made her admit she wanted him. Out loud, so she could hardly deny it now.

Did she even want to?

Think it through.

In no more than two or three weeks Marc would return to his law practice and his apartment in Richmond. He might come out here for the occasional weekend, but it was really too far from the city to be a convenient weekend retreat. So . . . even if they became lovers, time would end it eventually. Gradually, inevitably, he would be occupied by his busy life in the city.

Inevitably, there'd be no room for her.

Josie felt her lips twist in a painful smile. Ironic. She had no room in *her* for the consuming demands of a love affair, no emotional energy to spare, but if she gave in to what he made her feel and accepted at least the overwhelming physical passion he offered, it would very likely be the demands of *his* life that would ultimately end it.

Give him the benefit of the doubt and say he really wasn't interested in a brief affair; his definition of "lasting" could be anything more than a long weekend. And certainly, no matter what aberrant fixation he'd developed on her, it was highly unlikely that a dramatically handsome, sinfully charming, and irresistibly sexy lawyer would be at all interested in someone like her once he could return to his normal life.

The thought of endings hurt, and Josie told herself sternly that it shouldn't. They were both adults, after all. Both past the age of disguising perfectly normal and healthy lust beneath the pretty wrappings of euphemisms. He wanted her; she wanted him; and there was certainly a spark between them.

So—why not? As long as they were both responsible, as one had to be these days, and as long as both of them understood that nothing lasting would come of it, then . . . why not?

She forced her mind into a matter-of-fact mode. Being responsible, now, that might prove difficult under the present circumstances. She certainly hadn't come out here prepared for an affair, and she doubted that Marc had. Of course, after last night Marc could have no doubt that he would, eventually, wind up in her bed, and he was undoubtedly a responsible man. And his friend the doctor was visiting him now, and doctors were rabid on the subject of protection.

As they should be.

Her matter-of-fact mode slipped away, and Josie sighed a bit raggedly. Why did it all have to be so complicated? She didn't want to *feel* anything, not deep inside where all the painful, raw emotions already lived, taking up so much room and demanding so much of her energy. All she wanted to feel were the simple physical pleasures of a healthy young body.

And why did that seem so wrong?

She put the legal pad facedown on the couch and left the parlor, taking her coffee cup back to the kitchen. Not because she needed the caffeine, but because she simply needed to move. Her restlessness drove her to move about the house aimlessly with another cup of coffee, until she was drawn to a front window by the crunch of gravel.

The Jeep was leaving—with two men inside. The doctor friend was apparently taking Marc somewhere. For the first time Josie wondered where Marc's car was. Surely he hadn't been out here without a car?

When the Jeep was gone, she felt unexpectedly lonely. Even when Marc hadn't been with her, she had been aware of his nearness just across the garden in the cottage, and apparently she'd gotten used to it during the last week. Only a week . . .

She got a grip on herself. What time was it? A little after noon. Lunch first, and then she'd study the last couple of chapters of Luke Westbrook's biography and try to figure out what he wanted of her.

It was around four that afternoon that Josie's phone rang, startling her. The phone number here was unlisted, and she'd given it only to the school where she'd taught in case they needed to get in touch. Then she reminded herself that Marc undoubtedly knew the number, and besides, it was probably just somebody misdialing.

"Hello," Marc replied cheerfully to her guarded hello. "Have you missed me?"

She considered pretending she didn't know it was he, but discarded that for the next best thing. "Oh, have you been gone? I hadn't noticed."

"Now you've cut me to the quick," he said, nonetheless sounding completely unperturbed. "In fact, I'm so hurt I just may take back my offer."

"What offer?"

"Chinese takeout. I'll be leaving Richmond shortly, and thought I'd bring home Chinese take-out. But that was before you insulted me."

"Touchy, aren't you?"

"Sensitive. The word is sensitive."

"I suppose you want me to apologize?"

"I am," he said, "willing to forgive."

"Well . . ."

"Waiting patiently to forgive."

Trying not to laugh, Josie said, "I'm terribly sorry I didn't notice you were gone today."

Silence. Then, Marc said, "That lacked something."

"Oh? Like what?"

He sighed. "Anything to stroke my ego."

"Was *that* what you wanted? I thought you just wanted an apology."

"Do *you* want Chinese takeout?" he demanded awfully.

She caved in. "I'm sorry. Really and truly sorry. And, actually, I noticed you were gone all day. I even noticed you leaving. In a nice Cherokee with someone I presumed was your doctor friend."

Gratified, he said, "Do I hear a longing for egg rolls in that dulcet voice?"

It was Josie's turn to sigh. "You're an evil man. Don't forget those little things with the crab meat and cheese inside."

"No Chinese meal would be complete," Marc told her solemnly, "without those little things with the crabmeat and cheese inside. I should be there between six and seven. Good enough?"

"I'll be here."

"One day," he said casually, "I'll tell you what it means to me that you're there. See you soon."

Josie listened to the dial tone for a moment, then cradled the receiver. How was it possible, she wondered dimly, that a few words spoken casually could make her go hot and then cold with strange, shivery sensations she'd never felt before? And, dammit, why did she want to cry?

Slowly, she went back to the couch where she'd been making notes on a fresh legal pad. Notes about Luke Westbrook's death and the months leading up to it.

"Mmaaarrc?"

"Yes, he's coming home," Josie replied absently. Then she looked at the cat, who was sitting squarely in the middle of the coffee table, and frowned. "Stop doing that. I know you can't possibly be saying his name, but stop it."

"Yaaah," Pendragon agreed amiably.

"I wonder if this is what he meant about you doing uncatlike things. Have you been talking to him, cat? Have you been saying my name to him?"

Pendragon blinked and sort of murmured a little sound that had no discernible meaning.

Josie rubbed her forehead fretfully, then shrugged the matter off. Talking cats. What would be next? Not mysteriously moving keys, anyway, not if she had anything to say about it. She fished the little brass key from the pocket of her flannel shirt and stared at it. Since last night, the blasted thing hadn't been out of her possession. She'd put it under her pillow while she slept and had been carrying it around all day.

But what did it mean?

She looked at the notes she'd made, and they were just as unhelpful. According to his publisher, Luke Westbrook had exhibited no signs of depression in the months before his death. Oh, he'd been moody, sure, but no more than was usual for him. Secretive about the manuscript he'd said he was working on, and that was normal too. For him. He'd been a secretive man in many areas of his life.

The police had found the ashes of burned papers in the fireplace of the front parlor, enough for a good-sized manuscript; his publisher verified the fact that he was in the habit of burning anything he was displeased with. Forensic techniques then had not been much to shout about; the ashes had been sifted to look for unburned pages, but none had been found. Luke had been thorough in his destruction.

He had, apparently, shot himself through the left temple with a handgun from the collection he'd kept in his study. Had, apparently, fallen backward; he'd been found with his head on the hearth, the gun inches from his fingers. The police had been satisfied that the wound was self-inflicted, and Luke had left a suicide note.

His biographer had reproduced the note, verbatim, and Josie opened the book to read it as she had read it already several times. It certainly sounded like the last gasp of a deeply disturbed man, she thought. Rambling, disjointed sentences that attempted to explain why he couldn't live if he couldn't write. Why he couldn't trade on past glory. Why his life was so obviously worthless. Self-pity and paranoia. Bursts of irrational rage directed at a mysterious "they" who had "fed like parasites" off the work he had produced.

Josie found that part of the note particularly jarring.

Who were "they"? His publisher? Critics? That didn't make sense. As the biographer noted, his contracts had been fair from the beginning and lavish toward the end when his sales had climbed into the stratosphere. Luke had certainly never complained publicly—or privately as far as anyone could say. As for critics, they had adored his work; not even his first book had been trashed, as first books often were.

The police had noted the apparently groundless accusations and had shrugged. The man was unbalanced, of course—why expect his suicide note to make sense?

The biographer had, sadly, accepted this wisdom. He quoted Dryden. "Great wits are sure to madness near allied." Luke's genius had finally driven him over the edge. It had been known to happen.

Josie pursed her lips at that, as she had the first time she'd read the biographer's sad conclusion. Well . . . maybe. Though creative genius *had* been known to manifest peculiarities throughout history, Josie couldn't recall many writers who'd gone that way. Drank themselves to death, yes. Even killed themselves with guns and the like—but out of depression, not actual madness.

The letter read like madness.

She brooded about it for a while, but arrived at no satisfactory conclusion. It must have been suicide, despite her doubts. There was certainly no reason to suspect anything else. No indication that Luke hadn't been alone that final night. Neighbors, admittedly not close by, had heard nothing suspicious. Luke's brother—Marc's grandfather—had discovered the body the following afternoon when he'd come to visit.

And . . . was any of that important?

Absently checking her watch, Josie saw that it was after five. Between six and seven, he'd said. For no reason she was willing to explain to herself, she decided to take another shower and change clothes.

She took the key with her, hanging it on the shower nozzle and looking at it from time to time, once while shampoo was in her eyes. Afterward she dried herself and the key, then took it with her into the bedroom to dry her hair. Then, deciding that enough was enough, she put the key in her jewelry box and closed the lid.

"There. See if you get out of that." For good measure, just in case Pendragon was responsible for the key moving merrily about the house, she put the jewelry box in the top drawer of the dresser underneath her lingerie. See if it got out of *that*.

She left her hair loose rather than confined in its usual braid, and brushed it until it shone in the lamplight of the bedroom. After another quick decision that she didn't let herself think about, she put on a white satin camisole instead of a bra, not very unusual for her since she hated bras and loved silky things next to her skin. The matching panties were wispy and delicate.

Instead of her usual jeans, she pulled on a pair of brushed cotton slacks in a pale gold color, extremely soft to the touch and very close fitting. And instead of her usual sloppy sweatshirt, bulky sweater, or overlarge flannel shirt, she picked out the prettiest blouse in her closet. It was cream-colored silk, with long sleeves gathered tightly at the cuffs and an open V neckline. She tucked the blouse in and wore a wide leather belt that emphasized her small waist.

Without pausing to look into the mirror because she knew she'd lose her nerve, Josie slid her feet into dorm socks—the only thing chosen for pure comfort—and left the bedroom without bothering to turn off the lamp on the nightstand.

Trying not to think too much but very conscious of how nervous she was, she went downstairs to the den. She built a fire in the fireplace and fed Pendragon when he reminded her politely that it was his suppertime. She returned to the den and stood gazing around, and frowned when she noticed the box of books pushed into the corner by the shelves.

Damn, she'd forgotten all about that.

The tape was frayed and easy to rip away, but Josie grimaced at the dust. Great—and her in a silk blouse. She didn't bother to study the titles of the obviously old hardbound books, but quickly and gingerly placed them on the shelves. She'd look at them—and dust them—later, she decided. Right now all she wanted was for the shelves to look neat.

The empty box went back down the cellar steps, to be dealt with some other time. She got the percolator ready but didn't plug it in, made sure there was iced tea—which she drank winter and summer—and milk.

Restlessly wandering, she turned on the front porch light. She considered bringing her radio into the den, but turned the television on instead and forced herself to sit still on the couch and stare at the news.

Pendragon leaped onto the back of the chair he had claimed as his own, made a brief catlike comment—but nothing remotely resembling a "meow," which had yet to escape his lips—and settled down to wash up after his supper.

When gravel crunched, Josie got up, slowly, and went to the front door. When she opened it, he was already coming into the circle of light, stepping onto the porch, carrying the bag of Chinese takeout. He looked even more handsome than usual in a dark business suit with the silk tie loosened. Doing things in Richmond, obviously.

The cast was gone.

"Hi," she said.

"Wow," he said.

SEVEN

They ate the food casually, out of paper cartons in the den, both of them sitting on the couch. Marc had discarded his jacket and tie, and turned back the cuffs of his white shirt a couple of times; his left arm was just slightly thinner than his right, and Josie could see a pale scar beginning on his forearm and disappearing underneath the sleeve, but he used the hand and arm easily and was obviously glad to be rid of the cast.

"I knew Neil had tacked on a couple of extra weeks when he told me how long I'd have to wear the thing, just to annoy me," he told her in a satisfied tone as they were finishing the meal and she finally asked about the cast. "He didn't admit it, of course, but when I told him either he'd take the damned thing off or I'd find a saw and do it myself, he gave in."

Amused, Josie said, "Maybe he just didn't want you undoing all his hard work."

"That's what he said." Marc grinned at her. "Anyway, I promised him I wouldn't go back to work for at least two more weeks if he'd take me into Richmond, get the damned cast off, and release my car."

"Release?"

"It was sort of being held hostage. Neil knew if I had it here, I'd drive it—probably back to Richmond—so he either bribed or blackmailed Tucker to keep it in his garage until he decided I could have it back."

"And Tucker is—your writer friend?"

"Yeah. Tucker Mackenzie. And Neil is Dr. Neil Ferris."

Josie's eyes widened. "Good heavens. I've read Tucker Mackenzie's books; he's very good. And isn't Neil Ferris a rather famous sports doctor?"

"He's an orthopedic specialist, so he gets quite a few customers from the sports world. Plus, of course, the occasional friend smashed up on a highway."

His rueful tone made Josie smile. "He sounds like a very good friend. Both of them, actually."

"Yeah, they are. And both are dying to meet you, by the way."

"Me? But—"

Marc went on as if he hadn't heard her startled words. "To be perfectly truthful, I think Neil was less impressed by my threat than he was by my plea; I told him a man needed both arms to make love to a woman—and he agreed."

She didn't know what to say. From the moment she had looked at him at the front door, her nervousness had vanished; she didn't know why and didn't question it. All she did know was that she had never in her entire life felt so alive, and that it was because of him. Everything inside her seemed . . . poised somehow, waiting for something.

Marc set his glass on the coffee table and then leaned back again, watching her very intently. But he still sounded casual when he went on, "Neil's happily married, by the way. Tucker is dangerously single, which is why you won't be meeting him anytime soon."

She shook her head a little, puzzled, and Marc smiled. "He could charm the devil out of both cloven hooves and two prongs of his pitchfork—and I'm not nearly sure enough of you to take that chance."

This time Josie felt heat rise in her face. *Dammit, he's got me blushing like a teenager!* "Marc, I—"

"I wish I were sure of you. I wish I could tell Tucker or any other man that this incredibly beautiful woman with hair like fire and glorious eyes that haunt my dreams didn't care about anyone else. Didn't notice anyone else. Just me. I wish it more than I can begin to tell you. I don't know that. But I know you want me. And I think . . . you made up your mind today, didn't you?"

She didn't pretend to misunderstand. She tried

a little laugh that emerged shakily. "My mind? What has my mind got to do with it?"

"Everything." He moved closer, but still didn't touch her. His voice was quiet and slightly husky. "Josie, I left last night because I wanted you to have a chance to think, to be sure. I don't want you to wake up in the morning and kick me out of your bed."

"I wouldn't do that," she murmured.

"So—there is room for me?"

She nodded, slowly but without hesitation. *In my bed, yes.* In her mind, she stopped the answer right there, refusing to look any deeper. The part of her where the pain lay, where it took so much of her, was firmly closed off, and she wanted it to stay that way, at least for a while.

Probably, she thought, if Marc even realized she refused to allow the prospect of physical intimacy to touch her deeper emotions, he wouldn't consider anything missing. Probably, by then, he'd be back in Richmond and would be grateful she wasn't a clinging sort of woman. Probably, they'd even be friends after it was over.

Probably.

He leaned toward her, his left hand lifting to brush her hair away from her temple and then cup her cheek. She felt herself quiver and knew he saw it, felt it. She couldn't stop the reaction or hide it. She responded to his touch as if every cell in her body had been created to match him on some primitive level she could never understand.

For a moment, her dazed mind acknowledging the inevitability of her response to his slightest touch, what Josie felt was pure panic. It was too much, too intense, terrifyingly unconditional. *Just* desire? Oh, God, what a joke!

"Don't." He was closer, only a breath away, eyes darkened and heavy-lidded as they stared into hers. His face was hard with the look of control, and his voice was so deep it was nearly a growl. "Don't be afraid of this."

Josie didn't know what she might have done if he hadn't kissed her then. She might have pulled away, run away. She might have, somehow, found the strength to save herself. But once his hard, warm mouth closed over hers, she was lost.

Heat exploded inside her, rushing through her veins until even her skin burned feverishly. Her heart pounded wildly, out of control. She heard a faint moan and knew it came from her, knew that her entire body swayed toward him mindlessly. Her hands lifted, touching his chest and sliding upward, around his neck, her fingers tangling in his thick, soft hair.

Marc's arms were around her, crushing her against him with a force that stopped just short of pain and only fed her hunger. His mouth plundered and possessed, the thrust of his tongue shattering in its raw need, and Josie responded with the same urgency.

He lifted his head at last, breathing harshly, and for a moment his eyes burned like molten silver. Then he was pulling her to her feet and, just as swiftly and easily, swinging her up into his arms.

"You shouldn't—" Her voice was dazed, but she had to make a vague protest because she felt sure he shouldn't be carrying her with his arm just out of a cast, for heaven's sake, even if it did seem incredibly easy for him. "I mean—I can walk."

He kissed her again, briefly but with undiminished hunger, then laughed a bit roughly as he carried her up the stairs. "If you're worried about me, don't. I could carry you for miles. Besides, I don't want to let go of you."

Josie might have forced herself to protest again, but by then he had reached her bedroom and there was no need. He lowered her slowly to her feet beside the wide bed, his hands settling momentarily at her waist, and in the lamplight his expression was absorbed.

"God, you're beautiful," he said simply, looking at her upturned face as if he were memorizing every feature. "You make me feel like a teenager with raging hormones and precious little control, so wild for you I can barely think straight. When I saw you standing in the doorway tonight, I wanted to make love to you right there."

She wanted to say that she wasn't beautiful at all but that it was wonderful of him to say so, but he was kissing her, his hands framing her face as if she were trying to escape him, and words didn't seem important. His mouth teased now instead of demanded, arousing without force, and again, her body responded so quickly and completely it was as if she obeyed an instinct older than the caves.

"It feels like I've wanted you forever," he murmured against her skin, pressing feather kisses over her face. His hands returned to her waist, unbuckling the wide belt and casting it aside. The tail of her blouse was pulled free of her pants, and he made a rough sound when his hand slipped underneath to touch the satin camisole.

With her arms around his neck, Josie almost absently unbuttoned the tight cuffs of her blouse. Her eyes had been closed, but she opened them when he drew back far enough to concentrate on unbuttoning her blouse, and she watched his intent face as the camisole became visible.

When the blouse had been shrugged off and tossed aside, Marc made another of those low, uneven sounds as he stared down at her. The white satin molded her small breasts, gleaming in the lamplight with every quick breath she drew, and her nipples were clearly outlined by the sheer material.

Josie felt oddly more exposed than she would have been stark naked, and more female than ever before in her life. She thought it was the way he looked at her, with that utter absorption, the way his gaze so intently watched the rise and fall of her breasts. And then he lifted a hand, his fingers pressing, lightly stroking between her breasts, so that the satin provided a sensuous friction, and she thought her very bones quivered.

"Marc." It was barely said and all she said, all she could say, but it was pleading.

For a moment his hand remained still, and then it slid downward slowly until his fingers reached the waistband of her pants. He was looking at her face now, holding her eyes with his while he unfastened her pants and pushed them down over her hips. Automatically, she stepped out of the pants when they pooled around her feet, nudging them aside and somehow getting rid of her dorm socks at the same time.

"Touch me," he murmured. It was not a command but something urgently necessary.

She didn't think she was breathing and didn't know how she was standing, but when he lifted her hands and placed them on his chest, her fingers were astonishingly nimble as they unbuttoned his shirt and pushed it over his shoulders. Then those same deft and avid fingers were sliding over his chest, probing thick, springy black hair and hard muscles.

She leaned toward him and pressed her lips to him while her hands explored his ribs and hard belly. She blindly found his belt and got it unbuckled, but Marc stopped her before she could do more.

"If you go any farther right now," he told her huskily, "I won't be able to take it." He leaned over to throw back the covers of her bed, then lifted her and placed her in the middle.

Pausing only to get rid of his shoes and socks,

Marc joined her on the bed. He didn't completely undress for the simple reason that he was afraid he'd lose control; he wanted to go slowly, to look at her and touch her and taste her until the aching need in him was at least partially satisfied. But just looking at her had him on the fine edge of his control.

Her lustrous hair spread out around her on the pillow, the vibrant red burnished with the lamp's soft glow, and her eyes were darkly purple, wide and fixed on his face with a wondering kind of intensity. Her body was creamy pale against the dark floral sheets, the delicate white satin underthings she wore incredibly erotic for the simple reason that they hid very little and yet . . . enriched her natural beauty.

He'd grown so accustomed to seeing her in bulky sweaters and tops that he'd almost stopped thinking about how petite she was, and now her delicacy enthralled him. Not too thin, she was tiny, fine-boned and exquisite.

He leaned over her, easing the hem of the camisole up gently with his fingers until he could press his lips to her silky stomach. She quivered at the touch and he heard a sharp intake of breath even as her fingers slid into his hair.

"Marc . . ."

Just as it had before, her soft, husky voice saying his name, just his name, was almost enough to shatter his control. He was suddenly wild to see her completely naked and he knew his fingers were shaking as he grasped the hem of the camisole. She helped him get it off her, then clutched at his shoulder with a muted whimper when he touched her breasts.

Small and firm, they fit his hands perfectly, the coral nipples tightening even more when he touched them. His fingers and lips caressed her, learned her. Her skin was pure heated silk under his touch, and Marc thought he'd never be able to get enough of her.

But the urgency, in him and in her, demanded, and he had to obey. He stripped away the pale, wispy panties and eased her legs apart. Her thighs tensed when he stroked them, and he wanted to tell her again how beautiful she was, how wildly exciting, but he couldn't seem to find the words. Instead he touched her gently, his fingers sliding into red curls, probing until he found the moist heat of her.

Josie caught her breath and tensed even more as his mouth caressed her breasts and his fingers stroked her. She couldn't believe how incredible it felt, and she still found it impossible to say anything at all. Her fingers were in his hair, holding him. Faint sounds of pleasure escaped her, welling up from somewhere deep inside her.

Just when she was convinced she was going to break into a million pieces or melt into a puddle of liquid want, Marc rolled away from her and swiftly removed what remained of his clothing. She watched him dazedly, unable to say anything or move, or do anything at all except wait for him. She saw that she'd been right about him being a responsible man, and she was vaguely grateful to him for assuming that responsibility, because all she'd been able to think about was having him.

He returned to her before the sharp tension in her had time to ebb, and she caught at his shoulders in mute need when he spread her legs wide and slipped between them. She was ready for him, more than ready, but it had been a long time and the inexorable penetration was so shatteringly intimate that it shocked her. She stared, wide-eyed, up at his taut face, saw the intense pleasure and heard his low groan of satisfaction when her body sheathed his completely.

Then he was moving inside her and Josie nearly cried out at the sensations. The tension inside her wound tighter and tighter, burning and aching until she wanted to sob with it, until she felt like a single raw nerve stimulated beyond bearing. It was wonderful and dreadful and so sweet she couldn't believe she'd existed all these years without *knowing*, and if it didn't stop soon she knew she'd scream or turn into some kind of wild animal or just splinter into shards of pure raw need.

When the culmination finally came, it caught her completely by surprise, and she did cry out as waves and waves of throbbing ecstasy flooded over her. She was still caught up in the fiery wash of pleasure when she heard Marc groan harshly, felt him shudder under the force of his own release, and then felt herself drifting into blissful peace.

"You're a very silent lover," he said.

Josie didn't want to move. In fact, she didn't want to open her eyes, but pried them slightly open anyway to find him raised on an elbow and looking down at her gravely, something tender that was not quite a smile curving his lips. He had gotten them both under the covers, although she didn't remember it.

"Does it bother you?" she murmured.

"No."

She opened her eyes the rest of the way and looked at him more closely. "That sounded like yes."

He hesitated, then shrugged. "I guess I was wondering why. I mean, I would have thought you'd have plenty to say. You usually do."

Josie had to smile at that, but she nevertheless saw that his question was a serious one. Searching for words, she said slowly, "I don't know why, except . . . I felt so much. I've . . . never felt anything like that before."

"Never?"

"Never," she replied honestly. Compelled by something in his eyes, she added an explanation she'd had no intention of offering. "I—the only other man I've ever slept with was my high-school steady, and then just a few times before we went in opposite directions to college. We were just kids, and . . . well, I didn't think too much of the whole thing."

"Sex?"

Josie nodded. "I guess he didn't know much more than I did, or maybe I was just too young. Anyway, it wasn't something I missed afterward."

Marc smiled. "And now?"

She eyed him ruefully. "How do I answer that?"

He leaned down and kissed her, slowly and thoroughly, then murmured, "I'm not looking for a critique, sweetheart. I just want to know you'd . . . miss me if I went away to college."

Since the kiss had left her feeling dazed, it took Josie a moment to absorb and understand what he meant. Then, solemnly, she said, "I'd miss you very much if you went away to college. I'd probably call you every night and breathe heavily into the phone, and write you long letters filled with indecent suggestions, and climb the walls until Christmas vacation."

Chuckling, he kissed her again, briefly this time. "Good. A man likes to know he'd be missed."

Almost against her will, she said, "I knew from the first time I saw you that you'd be . . . memorable." Had he called her sweetheart?

Marc looked at her for a moment, then leaned down again and slowly pushed the covers to her waist, his mouth trailing downward between her breasts. "I wish," he murmured, "you'd said unforgettable."

Josie knew why she hadn't; not because it wasn't true, but because she was unwilling to admit to him that she knew she'd never forget him as long as she lived. But even if she'd been willing to correct her remark then, she wouldn't have been able to; just as before, desire was burning in her and she couldn't say anything at all.

Five minutes before, she would have sworn she lacked the energy to raise her head off the pillow, but by the time Marc pushed the covers lower, his mouth at her breasts and his fingers sliding down over her belly, her energy level had increased dramatically.

He made her forget everything except him and the way he could make her feel, carrying her away on a tide of sensation so intensely overwhelming she was almost afraid of it. Almost. But her body, it seemed, had surrendered at his first touch, and that was something Josie simply couldn't fight— even if she'd wanted to.

And she no longer wanted to.

Vaguely remembering that her silence had seemed to disturb him, she tried to say something while hunger coiled in her body, but all she could manage was his name, hardly more than a whisper of sound. It seemed to have a strong effect on him, which would have surprised her if her mind had been capable of thought just then, but since he chose that moment to enter her body with almost rough and urgent haste, she was too occupied with raw sensation to care about anything else.

There was no time for thought after that. All she could do was try to hold on to sanity—and even that slipped away from her at the end, when the pleasure peaked in a stunning eruption of ecstasy. . . .

"Yahhh."

She'd been drifting, Josie realized, already awake but unwilling to open her eyes. The feline greeting, unusually soft, roused her, and she opened her eyes slowly. The room was bright, which told her it was morning—probably around eight o'clock, though she didn't know for sure because Pendragon was sitting on the nightstand on her side of the bed, hiding the clock.

"Yahhh," he repeated, still softly.

"Hello," she murmured. There was an arm around her waist. She turned her head cautiously on the pillow, then pushed herself up on her elbows, still careful, so that she could see Marc better. He was asleep, on his stomach beside her with his left arm flung across her middle.

It was the first time she'd seen him asleep. His face was relaxed, the tautness of awareness eased. The dark crescents of his lashes hid his striking eyes, and the faint blue shadow of his morning beard softened and blurred the sharp angle of his jaw. She looked down at his left arm, at the scar that twisted up past his elbow. It would fade in time, like all scars, but right now it spoke of a great deal more pain than he had revealed.

He certainly didn't hesitate to use the arm. And for a man still supposedly convalescing, she thought wryly, he sure had energy to spare.

Three times. Three times during the night, he had awakened her with hungry kisses. And that had been after they'd finally fallen asleep sometime around midnight.

Josie had the uneasy suspicion that he had, during that passionate night, marked her indelibly as his. In fact, she was half afraid to look into a mirror, because she was sure she'd be able to see the mark.

Tearing her gaze away from him, she looked back at the black cat, who was purring loudly. "Why do I get the feeling," she murmured softly, "that all of this was somehow your idea?"

Pendragon blinked at her, then stopped purring, said, "Wow," and looked toward the doorway.

Josie followed his gaze automatically. She heard her own sharp intake of breath, but this time she was more startled than truly surprised.

Wow, indeed. Luke Westbrook, it was clear, disdained the notion that ghosts appeared only at night, and put paid to Josie's theory that after ten P.M. was his time to haunt.

He stood just outside the doorway, looking at her intently. He raised his left hand and, this time, beckoned urgently. Then he backed away, out of her sight.

Josie was on the point of waking Marc with an urgency of her own when she hesitated. What if she shook him awake and dragged him out into the hall to follow a ghost—and the ghost was gone? She'd look like an idiot—or worse. And Marc, who had at least been fairly neutral about her claims, might well begin to question her sanity.

She bit her lip, then slid carefully from the bed without waking Marc. Their clothing had been scattered about the room; the closest thing was his white dress shirt, and she put that on hastily. It smelled of him, a spicy male scent that made her legs go a bit weak and roused dizzying memories of his skin, of his body lying heavily on hers. . . .

With a tremendous effort, she got hold of herself. Luke. She had to follow Luke. She also had to roll up the sleeves of Marc's shirt several times and was still buttoning it as she padded barefoot out into the hall.

Luke was at the very end of the hall, at the door that led up into the attic. He beckoned again, and faded back through the closed door.

Josie found that sight more unnerving than anything yet, but she nevertheless obeyed his insistence and followed. She hadn't yet explored the attic in any depth; she had gone up once while settling in just to glance around, and had found a relatively small space under the rafters of the old house that was stuffed with old furniture, a few trunks, and other assorted junk.

Now, treading lightly up the narrow stairs, she wished she'd explored more carefully. The space was unheated, but not especially chilly this morning—but she wished she'd remembered her slippers or dorm socks because the floor was cold. It was fairly dark, the cramped space boasting only one small window curtained in some gauzy material that was almost in tatters. When she reached the top of the stairs and stood uncertainly, the gossamer curtains fluttered strongly, catching her eye.

Luke was nowhere to be seen.

Slowly, Josie approached the window. It was closed—nailed shut, actually—which didn't surprise her, because she hadn't felt a breeze. She pushed the dusty, filmy curtains wide open and looked out, assuming there was something important she was supposed to look for.

At first there seemed nothing unusual. The morning was bright, with fleecy white clouds drifting across an almost painfully blue sky; the trees waved their branches lazily; leaves, soaked by the recent rain, lay heavily on the ground.

Then, realizing that only this window was high enough to provide a view beyond the hills immediately surrounding the house, Josie looked farther out. Still, she saw nothing unusual—until a faint movement caught her eye.

Probably half a mile away, just beyond a hill

that would no doubt have provided a particularly good view of the house, a small figure appeared, trudging up a slope along a white rail fence. At the top, the figure turned and stood there for a long moment, seemingly gazing back toward the house. Then the figure bent, slipped through an opening provided by a missing board, and was soon lost among the trees.

"A woman." Josie didn't know why she was so sure, just something about the way the woman had moved. And something else, she thought, remembering the slight stiffness, the caution of movement. "An old woman."

But what does it mean?

There was nothing else out there, at least not that Josie could see. Nothing unusual. So it had to be the old woman. Luke Westbrook, dead for fifty years, had led her up here to the attic so that she could watch an old woman's morning walk. He had been urgent, so he must think it important . . . and Josie hadn't the faintest idea why.

Frustrated, she turned away from the window, intending to return to bed with Marc and try to convince herself she'd dreamed the whole thing. But as she turned, a shaft of bright light streamed through the open curtains and picked out the gleam of wood across the cluttered room in a corner near the stairs. A piece of furniture. A rather large piece of furniture, mostly hidden under a thick linen dustcover . . .

Josie didn't know why it looked so familiar,

why she felt so drawn to it. Not enough of it was visible for her even to identify it, and it was only when she went over and pulled back a corner of the dustcover that she realized she was looking at a desk.

A desk.

In a flash of memory, she suddenly recalled the portrait of Luke. He'd been sitting at a desk, she remembered. A big, heavy desk made of gleaming dark wood. And some of his furniture was still in the house, so why not that?

"Josie?" Marc, calling from downstairs.

"Up here," she called back, staring at the desk. There were things on top that had to be moved before she could uncover it completely, and she was wrestling with a rather large box—apparently filled with rocks, judging by the weight—when Marc reached the attic.

"What're you—"

"Oh, damn, *why* do people pack everything heavy in a single box?" she asked breathlessly.

Marc pushed her gently to one side and lifted the box without visible strain. "Where do you want this?"

"Oh—anywhere. I just need it moved." She was glad she'd stolen his shirt, because he looked awfully good bare-chested. She watched him set the box to one side on a trunk, then pointed mutely at the two remaining boxes on the desk. While he got those, she moved a dress form and an ancient sewing basket, which left the desk un-burdened by anything except the dustcover.

Marc came to her side, tipped her face up, and kissed her quite thoroughly and leisurely. Then he said, "May I ask why we're moving things around the attic at eight-thirty on a Wednesday morning?"

Josie couldn't help grinning a little at the infinite patience in his voice. "Well . . . I wanted to take a look at this desk."

"Why?" He was still patient.

She found that her hands were on his chest, that she was absently smoothing what was almost a pelt of black hair. "Nice," she said, without realizing she was going to.

Obviously realizing to what she referred, Marc said politely, "I'm glad you think so." He was smiling just a little, a very masculine smile.

Josie felt her cheeks burning, but said seriously, "You said some very nice things about me last night, and . . ."

"And now it's your turn?"

Realizing she was rapidly painting herself into a corner, she said, "Um . . . the desk—"

His hands slid down her back and curved over her bottom, easing her against him. "Never mind the desk. I woke up to an empty bed. It was a terrible and most unwelcome shock. My ego needs stroking."

She eyed him uncertainly. "I got the impression you had plenty of confidence."

"In most things," he agreed. "But I seem to be a mass of insecurity when it comes to you, sweetheart."

Josie was surprised. Somewhat rueful, she said, "One week after meeting, we're in bed together—and you're insecure? I can't imagine why."

"Humor me."

"Um . . . if you keep doing that with your hands, I'm not going to be able to say very much about anything. . . ."

Smiling, he continued to move his hands over her bottom. Almost casual but unmistakably intimate. The touch of a lover. "You look sexy as hell in my shirt," he told her.

Josie blinked. Already, the ability to utter anything coherent was slipping away from her. The effect this man had on her was terrifying. "I . . . um . . . was going to apologize. For stealing it."

"Don't. You can have every shirt I own, if you promise to wear them every morning. With nothing underneath."

Dazed, she felt a liquid warmth spread under his caressing hands and then slowly, gently, flow throughout her body. Her skin heated and her breathing quickened. And it wasn't gentle anymore. Her breasts felt full and hot, and between her legs was a feverish ache that made her instinctively press herself closer to him. Her head fell back, because he was exploring her throat with ardent lips, the scratching of his morning beard sensuous, and she heard a little whimper escape her.

As suddenly as that, as completely as that, she was lost, given over to him utterly.

Marc raised his head and drew a harsh breath. His hands grasped her waist, and he lifted her onto the edge of the desk behind her. Josie was hardly aware of what she was doing as she put her hands behind her to brace herself. He was between her knees, still kissing her throat as he unbuttoned the shirt she wore far enough to expose her breasts.

She felt her back arch when he touched her, and unconsciously gripped the dustcover beneath her as her fingers curled in sharp reaction. He was kneading and stroking her naked flesh, his mouth hot and hungry on her nipple, and she heard her own uneven breathing matching his, felt her heart pounding so hard she thought it would burst.

And it didn't matter. Nothing mattered except having him right here and now.

His fingers slid up her inner thigh and found her damp and ready for him. He groaned, and Josie answered him with a soft, uncontrolled sound of her own when he rhythmically stroked the most exquisitely sensitive nerves her body possessed.

She endured the spiraling tension, her head still thrown back and eyes closed, and moaned in relief when she heard the faint rustle of his clothing and felt his hard hips push her thighs wider apart. He entered her with a strong thrust of urgent need and Josie cried out in wordless pleasure, her legs closing around him and holding on tight, her back arching again.

The ascent had been so swift that the culmination could hardly be anything else. They were both caught in a current so strong that even if they had wanted to slow down, it would have been impossible. Together, perfectly in sync, they rushed to the peak, and over, and were left holding on to each other in the dazed aftermath like survivors of a storm.

Her arms around his neck and her face pressed against his throat, Josie gradually came back to herself. Her entire body was throbbing, echoing satisfaction, and for a long time she just luxuriated in it.

When she finally did draw back just a little and look up at him, Marc kissed her. "My God," he murmured.

Wondering if she looked as awed as he sounded, Josie shook her head. "What happened? Do you realize we're in the *attic*?"

He chuckled. "So we are. That'll teach you to wander off."

Briefly, she wondered why she had—but then remembered. "I had a reason," she told him.

"I know. You wanted to look at a desk."

Which she was sitting on. Momentarily distracted when he eased back away from her and reclaimed his pants, Josie paused a moment before saying, "Well, not exactly."

"Then what, exactly?"

Her shirt—his shirt—was gaping open. She closed and buttoned it, then got herself off the desk. With more than a little help from Marc; her legs were still shaking.

"I was lured up here," she told him, keeping her voice very matter-of-fact. "Help me get this dustcover off the desk, will you, please?"

"Lured?"

"The dustcover, Marc." She felt oddly reluctant to explain this to him. Maybe because they'd just made love rather spectacularly, or maybe only because she was afraid he wouldn't believe her.

But before he could ask the question again, Josie tossed back a corner of the dustcover to expose part of the desktop, and both of them saw the key. It lay there innocently, a small brass key with a faded loop of ribbon.

"That looks like the key you showed me," Marc said, a little surprised but not particularly disturbed. Because he didn't know, of course. He had no idea.

She picked it up slowly. Stared at it. The faded ribbon still bore faint water spots from where it had gotten wet in the shower. And here it was— underneath a dustcover that had been piled with heavy objects. Here it was, when it should have been in her jewelry box, in her dresser drawer, downstairs in her bedroom.

"Josie?"

"This was Luke's desk," she heard herself say

in a shockingly normal voice. "The one in the painting. The one in his study when he died."

She took a step back and looked at the desk. The center drawer, she saw, bore a small keyhole. When she tried the drawer, it was locked. Of course. And the key fit.

Of course.

Half-afraid there would be nothing, Josie slowly slid the drawer open. Inside was a leather-bound book atop a carbon copy of what looked like a manuscript, both lying beside a stack of letters tied with a faded ribbon.

Marc picked up the book and opened it. He looked at Josie quickly. "It's Luke's journal. The one the police never found when they were investigating his death."

Josie picked up the bundle of letters. There were many, all on blue stationery, the envelopes addressed simply, in a delicate, spidery hand, to Luke. They had never been mailed.

She held the bundle to her nose and, so faint it was three quarters imagination, smelled a woman's perfume. And that was when something clicked in her mind.

"Of course. *An old woman.*"

EIGHT

It took a while to explain, but Marc managed to get out of Josie the missing details and her thoughts regarding them. He knew she was reluctant because she was afraid he wouldn't believe her, and also because she was shaken herself by the nudging and leading that had caused her to end up unlocking the drawer of Luke's desk.

He didn't blame her for either reaction. And he believed it all. He believed it because he knew Josie well enough to be certain she was neither a liar nor delusional, but even more, he believed it because he loved her. Hell, if she'd told him black was white or up was down, he would believe her; he was that far gone.

In any case, he got the rest of the story out of her. The energetic activity of the key during the past days was explained while they showered, and she filled in the details of her trip up to the attic and the conclusions she'd reached, while he shaved and she dried her hair. By the time they had coffee and breakfast, and Marc had returned from a brief trip to the cottage to change into casual clothes, they were ready to settle down in the den and figure out the rest.

"If we can," Josie said, eyeing the manuscript, stack of letters, and journal now reposing on the coffee table. She had cleared away the remains of last night's meal while Marc had gone to change. "But it's been fifty years, and we don't even know what we're looking for, really."

Marc nodded. "So what if Luke was having an affair with someone named Joanna? He certainly never claimed to be a saint. And why he'd wait fifty years and then urge you to uncover his secret affair . . ."

"I know, it doesn't make sense. There has to be more to it. And . . . if that lady I saw out the window *was* Joanna, then all this must have something to do with her."

"It's a point to start from anyway. You know, just reading all this could take us days, maybe longer. What about your writing?" Marc asked, watching her much more closely than he showed —he hoped.

"Temporarily postponed," she answered, a bit too offhandedly to fool him.

He had a hunch about the "writing" Josie had come out here to do, and if he was right, then it was certainly understandable that she would grasp at any excuse to postpone her "work." Digging up the past, especially a tragic and traumatic past, was grim work even when one was detached—in this case something he doubted she could ever be.

"So you're . . . consumed . . . by something else now?" he heard himself ask lightly.

Josie looked at him, a bit startled at first. "Consumed? Oh. . . I did say . . ."

"That your writing consumed you, yes. Only now it seems to be these demanding Westbrooks who're . . . taking up all the room." He was still able to see her emotions, and so he knew that his comments disturbed her. And he wasn't much surprised when she chose to focus on the long-dead Westbrook rather than the flesh-and-blood man who had shared her bed last night.

Hurt, but not much surprised.

"Luke's mystery is surely a transitory thing," she said casually. "An interesting puzzle to try and work out. Once we find the solution, I doubt it'll . . . take up any room at all. Besides, I'm the one he's been haunting, and I feel honor-bound to try and help him."

"Admit it," he invited ruefully. "It's just as much Luke as it is the mystery that attracts you."

"Why do you say that?" she asked slowly.

"The way you say his name."

Josie frowned slightly. "How do I say his name?"

Marc wished he hadn't brought this up, but now that he had, he knew he had to finish it. "As if he's . . . someone you care about. Someone who matters to you."

She shook her head, then said, "I want to know why he can't rest in peace, that's all." She regarded him a bit uncertainly, then added, as if she couldn't let the subject drop so easily, "He *does* look a bit like you."

"Or . . . I look a bit like him?"

That brought another frown. "Marc, are you accusing me of having the hots for a ghost?"

He couldn't help but smile. "Not at all. If you tell me that I'm the one who turns you on, I'll believe it."

Josie sat down on the couch and murmured, "If you have to be told, after last night—and this morning—then one of us wasn't paying attention."

He had to laugh at that, and reminded himself that he had already more or less reached the same conclusion. He'd felt a stab of jealousy this morning when, after lovemaking so intense he had been totally staggered, she had seemingly been able to turn her attention so quickly to Luke's desk. But Marc had done some hard thinking, and the answers he'd come up with satisfied him.

A dead man was no threat to a living one, not when it came to love. Yes, Josie was interested in Luke—because he was a ghost, and because he apparently wanted her to solve some problem that had lingered fifty years after his death. That kind of puzzle would fascinate anyone.

But she was also, he had realized, using the mystery—perhaps not consciously—to occupy her mind. She had taken Marc into her bed, accepted him as her lover, and she seemed entirely comfortable with that fact—and with him. But it was obvious she wasn't yet ready to look beyond the pleasure they found together and admit there was more than passion between them.

If he hadn't known enough of her past to believe he understood what motivated her, the pain and wariness that urged her to try to protect herself, Marc would probably have driven himself crazy and her away from him by demanding the commitment he needed from her. But he was able —just able—to accept what she offered and wait patiently until she was ready for more.

At least for the moment.

And if, in the meantime, she wanted to concentrate on this apparent mystery, that was fine with him. He was with her, which was definitely what he wanted, and besides, it would—well, maybe—serve to occupy his own mind with something other than constant thoughts of her. And, truthfully, since it was his ancestor, he was more than a little curious himself.

So he had no business making jealous noises.

"I was paying attention," he told her solemnly, following her lead in lightening the discussion. "But I've told you how insecure I am about you. Hell, if I can feel threatened by a ghost, I'm really in trouble."

She let out a little laugh and looked at him with bright eyes. "I'll say. But if it'll soothe your ruffled feathers to hear it, you're the one I find sexy."

"I'm so glad." He grinned at her.

"Good. Now, do you think we might get started on all this reading?"

"I'll read the manuscript," he offered, sitting down on the couch beside her, "if you want to tackle the letters and his journal."

Josie had already untied the bundle of letters and held them in her hands, but she said, "I feel a little weird about this. I mean, if Joanna is the lady I saw this morning, still very much alive . . . isn't this invasion of privacy?"

"Arguable," Marc decided after a moment's thought. "Having been sent to him, found in his desk, presumably in his possession when he died, the letters belonged to Luke. And since this house and its contents now belong to me—the letters are lawfully mine."

She looked at him with a slight smile. "Okay, that's the legal answer. What's the moral one?"

"I was afraid you were going to ask that." Marc sighed. "Look, whether or not the lady you saw wrote these letters, we still have to read them. What choice do we have? We have to gather all the information we can before we can decide what to do. Right?"

"I suppose. But I feel like a voyeur."

Marc leaned over and kissed her, mostly because it had become a necessity to him. "Think of it this way. *If* there is a problem Luke wants solved, and *if* it does involve this lady you saw, then you just might be doing her a big favor by reading her letters."

Since she knew he was right, Josie sighed and began opening the letters to arrange them by date —oldest first. "What I can't figure out is why the police never found this stuff. I can't believe they wouldn't have searched his desk."

"They did search it." Marc had picked up the biography of Luke that they'd both read, and answered absently while apparently looking for a particular section. "I remember that mentioned in the police report. There were a few ordinary things in the desk drawers—none of them locked, by the way—but no manuscript or journal, and certainly no love letters."

"Then where were they? And how did they wind up locked in the desk fifty years later?"

"One of the things we need to figure out, I'd say."

Josie watched him. "What are you looking for?"

"There's a list of his published works. . . . Ah, here it is. I want to see if this manuscript ever became a book."

She waited while he scanned the list, then said, "Well?"

"Nope. Or, at least, not under this title. I suppose he might have changed it, but . . ." He put the bio on the coffee table and got the manuscript. It was tied up with frayed twine, and though the carbon type had faded, they could both read the title page.

"*A Sudden Death* by Luke Westbrook," Josie read out loud. "That's an ironic title, considering." She brooded for a moment, then asked, "Are you sure that's not on the list?"

"Definitely not by this title. Why?"

"I don't know. Yes, I do—it sounds familiar." Then before Marc could respond, she said dryly, "Of course, 'sudden death' is a sports term, isn't it? As in, sudden-death overtime?"

"Yeah. So it could seem familiar for that reason. Or just because it sounds like a fairly typical mystery title." Marc glanced at her, then indicated the upper right corner of the manuscript's title page. "Did you notice this?"

She leaned closer and could barely make out the faint numbers. "Four, thirteen, forty-four. A date?"

"I'd say so. Two days before Luke died."

"Does your friend Tucker date his manuscripts?" Josie wondered.

Marc was tempted to ask her if she dated her own writing projects, but it was a fleeting thought. "Like most writers these days, Tucker uses a computer, which automatically makes note of the day work was last done on a particular file. But he does note on his desk calendar when he begins and finishes a book. He says it gives him a stronger sense of completion."

They looked at each other for a moment, and then Josie said, "Maybe we'd better read awhile."

"I think you're right."

Was *A Sudden Death* a carbon copy of the manuscript Luke Westbrook had been supposedly unable to write before his death? If so, had he burned the original in his fireplace before committing suicide? And, if so, why? Why burn the original and keep a carbon if the project had caused him such anguish that it had driven him to kill himself?

Josie managed to push those questions aside for the moment, though it took an effort at first. However, by the time she had read the third letter from the lady named Joanna, she found herself completely caught up in that part of the puzzle.

Joanna wrote well—and she was a woman deeply, passionately in love with Luke Westbrook.

They had been lovers, that was apparent in the eroticism throughout the letters. It was clear the two had seen each other fairly often; she referred to those meetings in every letter, using phrases like, "yesterday when you smiled at me," and "last week when we met by the fence . . ." It was also clear that they had little time together; it seemed to be measured in minutes, and her joy when they could spend an hour or two with each other was so strongly expressed it was almost painful to read.

As a matter of fact, Josie found herself putting

the letters aside after the first dozen, because by then the reason their love affair had been secret became evident. Murmuring something vague about more coffee, she picked up her cup and retreated to the kitchen.

"Yahhh," Pendragon greeted her from atop a barstool.

"Hello, cat." She put on a fresh pot of coffee, then stood there leaning back against the counter and stared at nothing.

Married. Joanna had been married, and it appeared that divorce had been out of the question. And so . . . brief, secret meetings. Letters filled with passionate longing exchanged back and forth —Joanna frequently used the phrase "your last letter" in hers—and no way out of a situation that could have no happy ending.

Lord, what fools these mortals be.

Josie thought she could understand Joanna's willingness to risk so much for Luke Westbrook. People had, after all, risked much for love all through the ages. Usually women risked more than the men, mostly because of the ever-present possibility of pregnancy and the constraints put upon them by society, but who could say that men paid no price for illicit affairs?

Perhaps Luke had paid a price.

"Josie?"

She looked at Marc for a moment across the kitchen, then said, "They were lovers. Very discreet lovers. And Joanna was married."

Marc came toward her slowly. "Hence the secret affair."

"Yes. I'm not through with all the letters, but it seems pretty obvious that there was no question of a divorce for Joanna. I don't know why. Family pressure, religious reasons. Something. But not because she wanted to stay with her husband. She . . . she really loved Luke. And she believed he loved her every bit as much, that comes through."

"We don't know that he didn't." Marc smoothed a tendril of bright hair away from her face, then let his hand rest against the side of her neck gently. "You take things very much to heart, don't you?"

Josie shrugged, uneasy with his insight, and fought to ignore her body's response to his most casual touch. "I was just thinking that maybe Luke had more than one reason to kill himself. I was also thinking—what if it wasn't suicide?"

After a moment Marc said, "A jealous husband, you mean?"

"It's possible. Look, the letters span more than a year, and the longer something like that goes on, the more likely it is that the spouse will guess what's going on, or see something he shouldn't. Joanna lived nearby, that's obvious from the letters; she met Luke here at the house, but they also met out in the woods somewhere between this house and hers. Who's to say her husband didn't find out what was going on?"

"Then killed Luke and made it look like a suicide?" Marc wasn't disbelieving, just thoughtful.

"Why not? Or—why say it was premeditated? Why not a confrontation that ended up with Luke shot by one of his own guns? After that, making it look like a suicide wouldn't have been very hard. Write a passable suicide letter—on Luke's typewriter right there in the room—giving as his reason despondency over an inability to write, and then burn the manuscript found on his desk to make the motive seem more believable. Make sure the gun had only Luke's prints on it and . . . walk away."

Marc frowned. "I suppose he wouldn't have thought to look for a carbon of the manuscript. . . . But why didn't the police find the carbon and journal, and the letters?"

"That question stands—and begs to be explained—even if it was suicide." She felt discouraged. "And, dammit, how will we ever know? It's *Luke's* journal and manuscript, and letters written to him before his death, so we aren't likely to find an explanation as to what happened the night he died."

Marc looked down at her for a long moment and then said, "You really do believe Luke didn't kill himself, don't you? Why? What makes you so sure?"

Josie hadn't thought about it specifically, but when she answered Marc without hesitation, she realized her subconscious had already come to a decision. That didn't surprise her, but her fierce tone of voice did.

"Because suicide is cowardly—and the man Joanna loved, the man she gave herself to body and soul was not a coward."

Marc bent his head and kissed her.

"Um . . . what was that for?" she asked when she could, feeling a bit stunned.

"I wanted to," Marc replied simply. "Are you always such a passionate advocate?"

She got a grip on herself. "I don't know, I've never thought about it."

He smiled. "Listen, I have a suggestion. We've both been cooped up too much lately, and it'll probably do us good to get away and clear our heads for a couple of hours. Why don't I take you out for lunch, and then we can get a fresh start this afternoon. How does that sound?"

"It isn't lunchtime," she felt duty bound to protest.

"It will be by the time we find a decent place to eat."

"Well . . ."

"Fresh air, reasonable sunshine. And I'll let you drive my new car."

"Oh, well," she murmured. "If you're going to resort to nasty bribery. What kind of car? I haven't even looked out the window to see."

"A BMW. With all the bells and whistles."

"Really? In that case, let me find my shoes. . . ."

Leaning forward to drop the manuscript onto the coffee table, Marc said definitely, "I have read this before."

Josie looked up from the last of Joanna's letters and frowned. "How could that be? You said it hadn't been published."

"According to Luke's bio, it hasn't. Nevertheless, I've read the damned thing before. For the past hour I've been anticipating scenes—and *not* because they were obvious ones. Maybe Luke published it under a pen name at some point, and the biographer just missed it."

"You haven't finished the whole thing, have you?"

"No, I'm about halfway."

It was nearly nine P.M. that night, and they had spent most of the evening—with one lengthy interruption for more intimate matters—relaxed in front of a crackling fire, reading and discussing what they read.

"How can we find out if it's been published?" Josie asked. "Library of Congress?"

"I think I know a quicker way," Marc replied. "I'll call Tucker. It's a good bet that he's read practically every mystery written in this century, and he remembers plots, characters. If this story is as familiar to him as it is to me, he'll be able to track it down somehow."

"Will he be willing?"

"Sure. He loves a challenge. And he has his computer set up to get information."

"It's worth a try," Josie said.

Less than ten minutes later Tucker was saying, "*A Sudden Death*? Considering that murder is that, it's reasonable to suppose there've been at least a dozen variations of that title."

"Yeah, I know," Marc agreed, resting Josie's portable phone against his shoulder as he leafed through the manuscript. "But this is definitely Luke's style, and it just as definitely isn't listed in the bio as one of his books. So what gives?"

"A pen name, maybe, but—"

"But Luke never used a pen name, at least not according to everyone who knew him."

"Um."

"There are handwritten corrections on some of the pages; I'm not an expert, but the handwriting matches that in his journal—which neither of us has read yet."

After a thoughtful silence, Tucker said, "Give me a summary of the plot so far, and let me see if it sounds familiar."

Marc did so, keeping it brief but making sure he listed the plot points and the various characters.

"It's definitely familiar," Tucker mused when he'd heard it all. "List those characters again—by name. I'm writing this down."

When Marc had finished, he said, "What do you think?"

"Well, let's not jump the gun here. A hell of a

lot of mystery writers who came after Luke West-brook aped his style and stole his plots outright—maybe both of us are remembering one of them. But I'll see what I can find out."

"Great. Thanks, Tucker."

"Don't mention it. But you can mention something else. How're things with you and Josie?"

Marc glanced aside, where her bright head was bent over the last of Joanna's letters. "So far, so good."

"This little mystery of yours providing breathing space?"

"Something like that."

Tucker chuckled suddenly. "Definitely true love. You should hear how you sound—somewhere between guarded and besotted."

"Good night, Tucker."

"Good night, Marcus."

Marc turned off the phone and set it on the end table, just as Josie looked up and said, "Dammit."

"What?"

"I don't think my jealous-husband theory is going to work. In this last letter, dated two days before Luke died, Joanna says her husband, Roger, is coming home—the following month. From the war. Where he'd been, apparently, for two years."

"Since long before the affair began."

"Right. He was coming home because he was wounded, badly enough so that Joanna expected to have to go to an army hospital in Richmond to greet him." Parenthetically, she added, "Luke had already done his army service, hadn't he? I seem to remember something about it in the bio."

"Yeah, when he was just a kid—enlisted when he was seventeen. He was thirty-eight when he died."

"I think Joanna was a lot younger," Josie mused. "Midtwenties, maybe? Or even early twenties. She sort of reads that age. Anyway, her husband was coming home, wounded, and she was going to be waiting for him."

"Is that a . . . Dear John letter?" Marc asked.

Reluctantly, Josie nodded. "I'm afraid so. She was too afraid of her husband finding out about them to continue the affair, that's very clear. She had a three-year-old child, Marc, a little girl—that was why she didn't dare ask for a divorce. She knew her husband would get custody."

"I wonder if she had hoped . . ."

Josie nodded again. "That she'd be widowed. And the poor thing felt so guilty about *that*, she probably drove herself half-crazy."

Marc sighed. "What a situation."

Unhappily, Josie said, "Yeah. And it means that Luke probably did commit suicide. I mean, after this letter . . . He couldn't put the real reason in his note without destroying her life, so he could have invented all that garbage about not being able to write anymore—he probably didn't give a damn by that point."

"Burned the original of *A Sudden Death* but

wasn't thinking clearly enough to burn the carbon, which he'd put away somewhere," Marc said slowly.

"It makes sense. Dammit."

"We still have the journal to get through," he reminded her. "And that's really the only thing that might tell us Luke's state of mind that last week—assuming he made entries." He leaned forward and got it from the coffee table, then turned pages rapidly until he found the last entry. "Damn. The last entry is dated the tenth of April. Before he got Joanna's last letter."

"Of course he couldn't have made it easy for us," Josie noted dryly.

Marc closed the journal and put it on the coffee table, then leaned back and calmly pulled her over onto his lap. "Enough for today," he said. "Do you realize I haven't kissed you in hours?"

"Well, what have you been waiting for?" she demanded severely.

"Your undivided attention. And, now that I have it . . ."

The lamp-lit bedroom was quiet in the drowsy aftermath of passion, until it was disturbed by a giggle from Josie. Pendragon had leaped onto the bed and had attempted to get between them.

"You must," Marc told the cat, "be joking."

"Ppprupt," the big black cat responded.

"No way. She's mine."

"Waur," the cat said in obvious scorn.

"She is too. Tell him, sweetheart."

Josie was on the point of adding her grave agreement when it occurred to her that Marc was entirely serious. "Well . . ." she murmured.

Pendragon said, "Yah!" in a tone of derision practically in Marc's face, then turned and left the bed with dignity.

"Thanks a lot," Marc told Josie ruefully. "I've now had the incredibly disconcerting experience of having a cat judge my macho qualities—and give me a very low grade."

"I'm sure you'll be able to redeem yourself. Challenge him to a wrestling match," she responded innocently.

Marc laughed, then pushed himself up on his elbow and looked down at her. His expression was suddenly serious, and there was something a bit hesitant in his eyes.

"Don't," she said before she could stop herself.

He didn't seem surprised. "Don't what, Josie?"

A part of her wanted to move away, even run away, but that was virtually impossible since she was lying in bed with only a sheet pulled up over her naked body and his naked body, and he was so close, the heat of him warmed her. . . .

"Don't ruin things," she said.

"How would I do that?" He didn't wait for her answer, but supplied his own a little flatly. "By asking why you couldn't even pretend to the damned cat that you belonged to me?"

"People don't belong to each other."

"No? I belong to you."

Shaken, she could only stare up at him.

He kissed her, a brief contact that nevertheless seemed to brand her, and his voice was rough. "I do. You think I'd be worth a damn with anybody else now? Even if I wanted to walk away from you, I wouldn't be able to. I love you, Josie."

"You can't," she whispered. "Not in a week."

"No, not in a week. A day, maybe two." His smile was slow and crooked. "Lady, I fell like a ton of bricks."

"You only think so, because—"

"If you're going to try to tell me I fell in love because I was bored," he said calmly, "forget it. That is probably the most ridiculous thing I've ever heard."

She had to admit, it sounded ridiculous put like that, but Josie was still finding this impossible to believe. And frightening. "You can't love me. And —and even if you did, I don't want—"

When her voice broke, he said, "You don't want love? How can anyone not want love, Josie? How can anyone not feel incredibly lucky to find love?"

"You don't understand," she whispered.

Marc hesitated, then sighed. "You're wrong, you know. I do understand. I understand that your whole world was turned upside down when you were eight years old. I understand that it tore you apart watching your father trying to prove to people that he wasn't a monster. I know it hurt when your mother walked out. And I understand how too many years of living with all of it has convinced you that you have to stand alone."

She was staring at him numbly. "How long have you . . . ?"

"One of my professors in law school liked to review old cases. Your father's was one of them." He would tell her the rest, Marc thought, about Tucker and the research—but not now. Now the only important thing was to get this out in the open between them so it could be dealt with.

"You mean, you knew from the first day who I was?"

He shook his head. "No, not at first. But it came back to me eventually. You must have gone through hell."

"He was innocent," she said fiercely.

"I know," he said matter-of-factly, and smiled a little at her shock. "Sweetheart, it was obvious to even a second-year law student that your father should never have been arrested, let alone indicted and tried. The truth is, the police couldn't find out who really torched that hotel, a shocked city was yelling for action, and a perfectly logical and businesslike insurance policy was knotted into a noose shaped to fit your father's neck. He could never have been found guilty."

"Not in the real court," she said, bitter. "Not by the law. But he was tried and convicted in the court of public opinion. And he was condemned in the same court."

Marc touched her cheek gently. "I'm sorry about that. Really sorry. But there's nothing you can do about it now." He waited, watching her intently.

It must have been a full minute before she said, "There is something I can do. I can build a case against the man who really set fire to the hotel."

"You know who did it?"

Again, she hesitated, but her voice was steady when she replied. "Dad gathered information until he died. Then I took over. I was in college, but there was time. Time to study everything, all the reports and articles and court documents—and Dad's own papers. That's where I found the answer, in his personal papers."

"The answer?"

She nodded jerkily. "The first thing I found was in his journal, a cryptic note using only a single initial to identify who he was referring to. It took time, but I eventually figured out who it was. Dad had a friend, a very powerful man with political ambitions. National political ambitions. But he had done something that could have destroyed those ambitions—left the scene of what turned out to be a fatal car accident because he'd been drinking—and he confided in Dad."

After a moment Marc said, "I've heard far weaker motives for one person to destroy another, but—it would have been his word against your father's if it ever came out. Why wouldn't he have been willing to chance it?"

"I wondered the same thing, but I've followed his career in the last few years, and I can connect him—sometimes obscurely, but connect him—to at least three other men who seemed to have been victims of . . . timely arson. In each case, I believe he benefited by the removal of someone who'd been giving him trouble or otherwise had gotten in his way; either they were tangled up in the arson investigations, or else they seemed to just fade away. And I believe he likes starting fires."

It might have been hard to believe, but Marc believed it. Over the years he had learned that sicknesses sometimes hid behind bland or influential faces, and that even smart people sometimes did the most incredibly stupid things.

"Who is he?" he asked.

This time Josie didn't hesitate. "He's a congressman—and not likely to go any higher because, I gather, his fellow politicians find him difficult to get along with. His name is Robert Lyons."

Marc didn't recognize the name, but that didn't particularly surprise him. "And you plan to build a case against this man? Alone?"

"I—I couldn't afford to hire the lawyer who handled my father's defense to help me, but he says that if I can assemble a convincing case, he'll take it to the district attorney in Seattle—because two hundred and thirty people died in that fire, and even twenty years later the file is still open.

"I believe I can do it. It's not going to be easy, because there are so many bits and pieces—newspaper articles and court documents, police reports, witness statements. But I have to try. I've given myself a year to try."

"Your 'writing,'" Marc noted quietly.

She nodded. "My writing. It's what I decided to say, if anybody asked, because I didn't want to talk about it. And because I thought it better not to talk about it. If it got out, what I was trying to do, Lyons might somehow get wind of it." She moved her shoulders in a little shrug. "Best not to take any chances, I thought."

He looked at her for a moment, then said, "So this determination to vindicate your father takes up so much of you there's hardly any room left?"

Josie knew what he was asking. "That's part of it. I—I haven't thought about much else in nearly ten years. At least, not until I came here."

"And when you came here? What then, Josie? What now? Do you really believe you can pretend there's nothing between us except sex?"

Fighting against what all her instincts had tried to tell her, Josie said, "I'm not pretending. I'm not."

"Yes, you are." His voice was quiet, but insistent. "You're pretending that we're having a simple little affair, that you can't feel more for me because there's no room left inside you to feel more. But that isn't the truth, Josie. The truth is, you're pretending you can't feel because it hurts too much to feel. Because you watched your father being abandoned by almost everyone in his life, including your mother, and you swore you wouldn't let anything like that happen to you."

NINE

"That hurt him worst of all," she whispered. "He expected his business associates to back away; rats deserting a sinking ship. But people he had believed were friends backed away, too, even after he was acquitted. Then relatives. And, finally—my mother. She didn't run to another man, she just ran away from him. He was virtually bankrupt, with hardly anything left except my college trust fund and a few stocks. Mother . . . she believed it, too, believed he'd killed all those people. You could see it in her eyes. He could see it in her eyes. It was what finally broke him."

Marc didn't hesitate. "Sweetheart, what happened to your father was a tragic thing, but you can't let it cripple you. You can't protect yourself from hurt by refusing to allow anyone close to you."

Josie wanted to argue that that wasn't what she

was doing, but she heard herself speaking in a far-away voice she hardly recognized as her own. "I learned the lesson. Then—and other times. There were so-called friends who looked at me strangely when they found out who my father was. There were the parents of friends when I was growing up, nice, ordinary people who didn't want their kids near me. And there were boys who . . . who thought that because my father had done such a dreadful thing, that I was . . . somehow an easy target. That I didn't have any feelings.

"Remember that high-school steady I told you about? We didn't break up because we went to separate colleges; I was accepted to his college, and that's where I was going. But then his sister told me . . . that he'd gotten another girl pregnant and had to marry her. He told me it had just happened, that it didn't concern me. He never even said he was sorry."

"He was a bastard," Marc told her. "That doesn't mean all men are."

"I know that. I also know that some people . . . just don't belong in relationships. Maybe it's bad luck or bad timing, or just the way things are."

"Josie—"

"It isn't *you*, don't you understand that? It's me. I'm not capable of—of feeling things deeply. Not anymore."

Marc framed her face in his hands. "Sweetheart, what you don't seem to understand is one very simple fact. I love you. I'm in your life, and I'm not going anywhere." He smiled. "As for you not being able to feel deeply, stop kidding yourself."

"I'm not—"

"My poor darling." He kissed her, his mouth tender. "You feel more than anyone I've ever known. And sooner or later you're going to have to face that. Sooner or later you're going to have to realize that none of us can stand alone. And when you do finally understand that, I'll be here."

When he reached to turn off the lamp on the nightstand and pulled her closer, Josie felt her body nestle against his as if obeying the simple need for sustenance. But her mind was troubled, and it was a long time before she slept.

If she hadn't been able to convince herself that what she felt for him was mere desire, she had at least been able to avoid looking for a more complex and far more frightening truth within herself. But now . . .

What did she feel? Desire, yes—dear Lord, yes. And interest, of course; he was a fascinating man with a sharp and active mind and a good sense of humor. And she felt a sense of . . . of what? Of kinship? They seemed to match each other somehow, and were content together in an easy way that Josie felt strongly was uncommon for new lovers.

All of which meant . . . what?

I love you. I'm in your life, and I'm not going any-where.

He couldn't really mean that. Could he? A man like him, who must have had women stepping on one another's toes to get close to him, falling for a pale, redheaded schoolteacher with a notorious last name and far too many shadows in her life?

Josie rubbed her cheek against him and felt his arms tighten around her. Odd, how safe she felt with him. Safe, really, for the first time in years. She hadn't even thought about her gun in days; was it even still in her purse?

She made a drowsy mental note to look in the morning, just to be sure, and felt herself beginning to drift toward sleep. He believed her father had been innocent . . . that was good. And he believed in the ghostly visits of his ancestor, even if he hadn't actually seen Luke himself. That was good too.

He loved her? Really loved her?

How remarkable . . .

"Does the name Colin Andrews mean anything to you?" Josie asked.

Marc looked up from his study of the last few of Joanna's letters and thought about it. "It's vaguely familiar, but I can't place it. Why?"

"Because, during the last few months of his life, Luke mentions this Colin several times here in his journal. He had a letter from Colin, he spent an hour or so with Colin, Colin told him—like that. It looks to me as if this Colin had dreams of being a writer, and Luke was having trouble telling him that he didn't have much talent."

"Didn't you say that Luke mentions corresponding with several young writers?"

"Yes."

"Then . . . ?"

In a careful voice, Josie said, "None of them had an appointment to come here and talk to Luke . . . on the evening of April fifteenth."

Marc sat up straighter. "What? According to the police, nobody came near this house on the fifteenth."

"I know. But if Colin kept his appointment, somebody was definitely here." She scowled down at the final entry of Luke's journal. "Dammit, if we only had one more piece of the puzzle. I wonder if this Colin Andrews is still alive."

"God knows."

Josie didn't blame him for sounding dismayed; tracking down a man they knew virtually nothing about after so many years was bound to be a daunting task. "*Somebody* must have known something, or else we couldn't have found all this stuff locked in Luke's desk fifty years after the police claimed they turned his study upside down and inside out."

There was a sudden thud from a corner of the den, making them both jump.

"Yaaah," Pendragon announced commandingly.

"Where is he?" Josie wondered, unable to see the cat.

"By the bookshelves." Marc's voice sounded odd, and his expression was a bit wary when he got up from the couch and went over to the shelves. He bent down, whatever he was doing hidden from Josie by a chair, and then straightened with a book in his hands.

"He knocked it off the shelf?" Josie frowned at Pendragon when the big cat jumped on the back of the chair—his chair. "That was clumsy of you, cat."

"Maybe not," Marc murmured.

"What do you mean by that?"

Marc didn't answer immediately. Instead he checked several of the other books on the shelf, opening each and looking at the flyleaf. "Josie, where did these come from?"

"The cellar. There was a box, all sealed up. I didn't think you'd mind if I brought them up here. I haven't had a chance to look through them, I just shoved them onto the shelves, but—" She frowned. "Why?"

"He never lived in this house," Marc said almost to himself. "But I suppose he stored things here, the way we all did. Packed them away and forgot about them."

"Marc, who are you talking about?"

He came back to the couch, carrying the book Pendragon had knocked from the shelf. "My grandfather."

"Those were his books?"

"Yes, according to the bookplates. And this is his journal, which I didn't even know existed. Nor, I think, did my father know, or probably anyone else. Just one more box of junk down in the cellar, until you found it."

"Actually," Josie offered slowly, "Pendragon found it. Or at least, he drew my attention to it."

They both looked at the cat, who was sitting on the back of his chair washing a forepaw.

"Cats can't read," Josie stated.

"No," Marc agreed. "Impossible. But . . . he did knock a book off one of the shelves at the cottage. And it just—coincidentally, of course—happened to be Luke's bio."

"Sheer happenstance," Josie decided after a startled moment.

"Absolutely."

"Woo," Pendragon murmured contentedly.

Marc cleared his throat and got back to the matter at hand. "Well, anyway, we have Grandfather's journal. It's lucky average people did more writing in those days."

"I'll say." Afraid to get too excited, she said, "He's the one who found Luke, isn't he?"

"He's the one. Cross your fingers and hope he managed to make an entry about that day. . . ."

They both bent over the journal, looking together as they searched for the relevant date. And it was several minutes later when Marc leaned back and looked at Josie.

"Well," he said, "at least now we have part of the puzzle solved. Grandfather was the one who removed the journal, letters, and carbon of the manuscript from Luke's study. After he found the body and *before* he went for the police. That was rather unlawful of him."

Josie took the journal and reread a couple of the passages. "He believed it was suicide. Thought it was more than despondency over the writing not going well. Luke had confided in him about loving Joanna—not mentioned by name here probably out of discretion, but certainly it was her—and had asked his brother to make sure that if anything ever happened to him, nothing . . . incriminating would be left lying around to harm the lady's reputation."

She looked at Marc and smiled a little sadly. "A different age. Or maybe you just had uncommonly gallant ancestors."

"A bit of both, I think." Marc shook his head, then said, "He doesn't say why he took the carbon, or why he didn't happen to mention it to the rest of the family."

"No . . . but it looks like this journal goes on for a year or so after Luke's death. Wait." She read silently for a few minutes, then looked at Marc.

"Got it. He found the carbon locked in Luke's desk along with the letters and journal, and put it aside intending to give it to 'Luke's lady' at a later time because he thought Luke would have wanted that—and he doesn't seem to have had any idea that the original didn't find its way into print. Do you think he thought it was an old manuscript? Is that possible, that he wouldn't know?"

Marc frowned. "Well, think about it. There's a suicide note claiming that Luke hasn't been able to write at all, which Grandfather might have believed to be at least partly true, burned papers in the fireplace, and no manuscript or notes on the desk. And he might not have read any of Luke's books; according to Tucker, the families of writers often don't."

"So he might not have been familiar enough with Luke's work to recognize an unpublished manuscript. I guess that makes sense. There would have been statements from the publisher?"

"Presumably. Grandfather was the executor of the estate, so he would have gotten them. But he probably wouldn't have noticed one title missing from the rest. And since, apparently, the publisher hadn't been notified that a manuscript had been finished, they wouldn't have asked about it."

"I guess stranger things have happened," Josie agreed, then read a bit more. "Um. It appears that Luke's lady went away not long after his death, and your grandfather didn't think she was coming back. He'd—what is this? Oh, I see. After deciding the house would be kept for the family, he had—he says 'disposed of'—most of the furnishings. But he had Luke's desk moved up to the attic, and he locked the journal, letters, and manuscript in the top drawer, intending to give everything to Luke's lady if he ever saw her again."

"Apparently, he never did."

Josie looked at Marc. "Do you suppose that's all Luke really wants of us? That we give this stuff to Joanna?"

"If she's alive and we're able to find her, you mean?" He shook his head. "I don't know, that sounds a little thin. I mean, why would he? Fifty years later?"

"Maybe she's just come back."

"Maybe—but the question stands. It's doubtful there's anything in any of this important enough to remind a—an old lady of a love affair that happened fifty years ago."

Before Josie could admit that he was right, the phone rang. It was on the end table on Marc's side, so she gestured for him to get it. "Besides, it's probably your friend Tucker."

It was Tucker, and he was excited. "Marc, read me the first few pages of that manuscript."

"Read them to you?"

"Yeah, verbatim."

Marc shrugged and obeyed, reading the first four pages of *A Sudden Death* over the phone.

"I'll be damned," Tucker said.

"What? Did you find this manuscript in print?"

"Oh, yeah. It was published in 1945. I'm looking at a copy. And you just read me the first four pages."

"Then why isn't it listed in Luke's bio?"

"Because," Tucker said dryly, "he didn't get the credit for writing it."

"What?"

"You heard me. *A Sudden Death*, which you described to me in correct detail and the first four pages of which you just read to me, was supposedly written by Colin Andrews. Who, curiously enough, published only that book—though he lived another ten years."

"How did he die?" Marc asked slowly.

"That's another curious thing," Tucker replied. "After practically drinking himself to death, he apparently decided the bottle wasn't fast enough, so he drove his car off a bridge. And he left a suicide note. Want to hear it?"

"I think so, yes."

"Okay. There's some rambling stuff at first, not of interest to us—and then he gets to the point. 'I can no longer live with the pain and shame of what I have done. In a senseless, malicious rage, I destroyed a life, and a genius. It was unforgivable, and I will not be forgiven.' "

After a moment Marc said, "I suppose the police drew their own conclusions."

"Yeah. Since it was without a doubt suicide, and since he was an author who hadn't written in ten years, they decided he was referring to his own genius having been cruelly destroyed by himself." Tucker paused, then added, "If it had been closer to the date of Luke Westbrook's suicide, somebody might have wondered. If Andrews had had any public connection with Westbrook, somebody might have wondered. As it was . . . ten years and half a country away, who bothered to find another answer?"

Who, indeed.

"Thanks, Tucker."

"Are you going to go public with this?"

"Would you?"

"Yes. Andrews didn't have any family to be hurt or embarrassed by it, and Luke Westbrook deserves to have the truth about his death known."

"I think you're right."

"Say hello to Josie for me. Bye, Marc."

As soon as he set the phone down, Josie said intensely, "If you don't *tell* me—"

Marc reached for her hand and smiled apologetically. "Sorry, love. It just kind of . . . floored me. It seems you were right after all. Luke didn't kill himself."

He reported Tucker's findings, including the quote from Colin Andrews's suicide note. "Tucker says he'd take it public, and I agree. God knows if we have enough proof to convince anyone other than the family—but at least we'll know the truth."

"I'm glad Luke didn't kill himself," Josie said. Then a thought occurred to her. "You know . . . if I had written a Dear John letter, and right afterward my former lover killed himself, I think I'd probably feel guilty. Very guilty. Maybe that's what Luke wants us to do—tell Joanna she didn't drive him to suicide."

"Yah," Pendragon said.

Marc looked at the cat, started to comment, and then apparently thought better of it. He looked back at Josie. "I'm game if you are. How do we find out if someone named Joanna lived around here fifty years ago—and might be here now?"

Josie considered that a minute, then smiled. "We call the nearest church and have a chat with the minister."

Marc returned her smile. "You're brilliant. No wonder I love you so much. Where's the phone book? Or—do they list churches in phone books?"

"It's over there on the lower shelf of that table. And, yes, they list churches. In the Yellow Pages," she told him dryly. "Another sad comment on the times we live in."

"I don't know," Marc said philosophically as he went to get the phone book, "maybe it's just efficiency."

"The watchword of modern times," she murmured.

Marc grinned at her and said, "You call. A woman looking for another woman is much more likely to meet with cooperation; I could be an ex-husband or a serial killer."

"Or a salesman," Josie offered more prosaically.

"Almost as bad . . ."

They had debated: call first, or just appear? Either way could be argued, and was, but it was already midafternoon and both of them wanted to meet Joanna. Just appearing won out over calling, mainly because there was too much to explain over the phone, and seeing—especially seeing Marc—might prove the easiest way to broach a difficult subject.

So they got into Marc's BMW and set out for Blue Meadow, a thriving Thoroughbred horse farm a few miles away that was in the process of being sold.

The minister Josie had reached on her third try had been elderly and very helpful. Of course he remembered Joanna Canfield and her fine husband, Roger. Why, hadn't he baptized their little girl—goodness, it must have been more than fifty years ago? Roger had been wounded in the war, and they'd moved away afterward because . . . yes, because he hadn't been able to ride anymore and couldn't bear being around the horses. His brother had run the place, and after that a nephew, and, yes, he remembered now that he'd heard the Canfields were getting out of the horse business. Selling the place, what a shame. Why, yes, Joanna had been in church last Sunday, so good to see her again. She'd come back to say good-bye to her daughter's birthplace and perhaps claim a few mementos. Then she would be returning to California, where she'd lived all these years even after her husband had died. . . .

Blue Meadow was indeed a thriving place, with neat white fences and, even this time of year, green pastures. The long driveway was straight between two such pastures dotted with horses; Marc took a fork that led to the sprawling house rather than stables, and when they reached it, he parked three car lengths behind a huge moving van.

As they got out of the car Josie murmured, "If we'd waited much longer, we might have been too late."

Marc nodded agreement and put a hand at the small of her back as they went up the walk. They had to dodge a moving sofa, human legs staggering beneath it, then found themselves peering through the open double doors into a foyer.

"Excuse us?" Josie called.

A slim woman of about thirty appeared, her jeans faded and blond hair caught back with a ribbon. She looked at the clipboard she carried, then at them, clearly harassed.

"If you're selling something—" she said warningly in a friendly but beleaguered tone.

"No," Josie replied, sticking with Marc's theory and doing all the talking. "We've obviously come at a rotten time, but—is it possible for us to speak to Mrs. Joanna Canfield?"

The blonde was frowning as she looked at Josie, a faintly puzzled where-have-I-seen-you-before expression in her blue eyes. But then she smiled. "Sure, I guess so. Come on—she's probably hiding out in the sunroom; it's the only place the movers haven't gotten to yet."

They followed her through the huge and mostly empty house to where French doors stood open to admit them to a bright, plant-filled sunroom. "Visitors, Gran," the blonde called out, and then, as an ominous crash sounded from the front of the house, added hurriedly, "Oh, damn, excuse me—" and abandoned them.

Joanna Canfield was probably in her early seventies, silver-haired and still beautiful. Slender and petite, she was casually dressed—in jeans. And looked good in them.

Boy, what Luke missed. Josie couldn't help shaking her head a little, but then went still as Joanna turned from her contemplation of a dwarf tree to greet them.

She had gentle, sad eyes in a milky-pale complexion with astonishingly few wrinkles. Her eyes were pale violet.

Josie, who had encountered very few people with eyes that color, felt surprise—and then more than surprise. She was almost certain Joanna's hair had been red in her youth. And there was more, an elusive familiarity. . . .

"Are we related?" Joanna asked immediately, her musical voice puzzled.

"No." Josie cleared her throat. "No, Mrs. Canfield, I don't think so."

That was when Joanna looked beyond Josie to Marc. It might have been fifty years, but clearly she had not forgotten. Her shock was obvious. "My God," she murmured.

Marc came forward quickly to catch her arm and ease her into a wicker chair, because it was fairly obvious she didn't trust her legs to support her.

"We should have called first," Josie said. "We're *so* sorry, really—"

Joanna shook her head a little, regaining control, and waved them to two more wicker chairs. She hadn't taken her eyes off Marc's face. "He had no children," she murmured.

Marc answered the unspoken question. "No, Mrs. Canfield, he had none. Luke Westbrook was my grandfather's brother. I'm Marc Westbrook. And this is Josie Douglas."

"I see." She drew a little breath and then seemed to realize how odd their visit was. "But—I don't understand. Why are you here?"

Josie glanced at Marc, then reached into her voluminous shoulder bag and drew out the ribbon-bound letters. "We . . . thought you'd want to have these, Mrs. Canfield. We were looking through the attic at Westbrook and—and found them."

This, too, had been debated, in the car on the way. Keep it simple, they'd decided. Play it by ear, but there was no need to bring Luke's ghost into it unless absolutely necessary. For all they knew, Joanna Canfield would sooner believe in fire-breathing dragons than ghosts, and there was no reason to make the lady think they were a couple of lunatics.

Joanna took the letters and held them, stared down at them. She didn't ask the obvious, if they'd read the letters, because the answer to that was evident. Instead she asked, "How did you find me?"

"The minister at Oak Grove Church," Josie replied. "We didn't tell him anything except that we were trying to find you, of course."

"Of course." She was still gazing at the letters, one thumb smoothing faded blue stationery.

Josie plunged ahead. "Mrs. Canfield, we found some other things, too, things Marc's family knew nothing about. Things that seemed to us . . . pieces of a puzzle. Luke Westbrook's journal. And a copy of a manuscript."

"His journal?" She looked at Josie then and shook her head. "And one of his books? I'm sorry, my dear, I don't . . . Why are you telling me this? It was all so long ago."

Ignoring the question, Josie said, "That's what made it difficult, of course, that it was so long ago. But we think we've finally managed to piece it together." Quickly, without giving the older woman time to interrupt, she explained about Colin Andrews stealing Luke's final book, and the suicide note Andrews had left that spoke of destroying genius.

Marc spoke then, saying quietly, "I'm going to make what happened that night public, Mrs. Canfield. I don't know how much I'll be able to prove, but I think it's important that family—and others who cared about Luke—know the truth. He didn't commit suicide."

There was a long silence and then, her eyes fixed on his face, Joanna whispered, "You're sure?"

"We're sure." Then he smiled. "Did he ever tell you what the Westbrook family motto is?"

"No."

"It's—Never Give Up. He wouldn't have, Mrs. Canfield. He didn't."

In spite of everything, Josie couldn't help shooting Marc a rueful look. If she'd known about that motto, she might have given in to his determination with a bit less of a fuss. One did not, after all, attempt to fight a family motto.

"I promise you," Marc said to Joanna. "He didn't commit suicide."

Very slowly, she returned his smile, and her lovely eyes no longer held the shadows of sadness. "Thank you. Thank you very much."

"We wanted you to know," Josie said. "And now we'll leave you in peace."

"Very much in peace," Joanna murmured.

Marc and Josie rose together, and Joanna looked from one to the other of them with speculation as she rose as well. "Are you two . . . ?"

"Yes," Marc said firmly. "We are."

"So," Joanna said, "Westbrook's finally getting its redhead. The house, I mean. He always said it would."

Josie looked at her for a moment, then said, "Mrs. Canfield, you wouldn't happen to be missing a pet, would you? A big black cat?"

Faintly surprised, Joanna said, "Why, no, my dear. I love cats, but I'm terribly allergic. Can't bear to have them around me. If you have one, it isn't mine."

"I was . . . just wondering," Josie murmured.

"It's almost enough," she said much later that evening, "to make you believe in fate. I mean, that I'd pick this of all houses to come to; that you'd be here convalescing; and that Joanna Canfield would return home. All at the same point in time. Like . . . like things converging. Almost as if there was a guiding hand."

She looked at Pendragon, on his chair, and frowned.

"Don't even think it, please," Marc begged

her. "This whole thing has been strange enough without supposing he had a part in it."

Pendragon opened one eye, looked at them, and said, "Yaaah," in an affable tone. Then he closed the eye.

Josie couldn't help laughing, but said half seriously, "If he goes away as mysteriously as he came, I'm going to convince myself he was a witch's familiar just stopping by on his way to Halloween."

"I'd be willing to believe almost anything by this point," Marc told her. "Especially now that Westbrook has its redhead."

It was a question, and Josie looked at him gravely. They had turned the lamps down low, and the firelight flickered over his handsome face and glimmered in the tarnished-silver eyes. For a moment she couldn't say anything, and he went on in the same calm tone.

"Making Luke's story public will be easy compared to vindicating your father. That'll take some tricky footwork. Are you going to let me help you? After all, you helped with my family troubles. And if there's anything I know, it's how to put a legal case together."

She knew what he was asking. And she knew that if she evaded the subject or put off deciding, Marc would simply wait. They would go on talking, and laughing, and making love. Tomorrow or the next day he would ask again, and if she was still not ready, he would go on waiting.

Never Give Up.

"You'll have to go back to your practice soon," she murmured, realizing only then, in that moment, that there had been much more room in her than she had ever guessed. Room for trust. Room for love. Room for Marc.

He shrugged. "Eventually. But Richmond isn't that far away; I plan to spend my nights with you. And my weekends. And as many afternoons as I can manage. I love you, Josie."

"That's a good thing," she heard herself say seriously. "Because I love you too."

For a moment he didn't move, a man fearful of breaking something precious. But then he did move, and she was in his arms.

"Thank God," Marc said unsteadily into her hair.

"Thank Luke," she said. And when he drew back to look at her, she said softly, "Marc, he came back from *death* to get somebody to tell the woman he loved that it wasn't her fault he died. Once I understood that, I knew how important love is, how much we need it. I knew I couldn't shut it out. I knew I didn't want to anymore."

He held her tightly for a moment, then rose and lifted her into his arms, and carried her toward the stairs.

But at the bottom of the stairs he stopped abruptly, and Josie realized he was staring toward the front parlor. She looked as well, not much surprised to see Luke there in the shadowy doorway. He was smiling at them. Then he gave a kind of bow, clearly gratitude, and faded back into the darkness.

Josie linked her fingers together behind Marc's neck and looked at his dazed face. "I told you," she said simply.

EPILOGUE

The cat remained until after Halloween. He stayed long enough to see them come home from an outing with glowing faces and shake rice out of their shoes. After that, however, he knew they could get along without him.

So he asked, one gray afternoon, to be let out the front door, and he thought they understood he wouldn't be coming back, because both of them said good-bye and watched him, he knew, until he reached the pine woods. Then they went back into their nice house, with its nice nooks and crannies.

And he went on.

THE EDITOR'S CORNER

    The end of summer means back to school and cooler weather, but here at LOVESWEPT temperatures are rising with four sensational romances to celebrate the beginning of autumn. You'll thrill to the sexiest heroes and cheer for the most spirited heroines as they discover the power of passion. They're sure to heat up your reading hours with their wonderful, sensuous tales.

    Leading our lineup is the marvelously talented Debra Dixon with **MOUNTAIN MYSTIC**, LOVESWEPT # 706. Joshua Logan has always been able to read anyone's emotions, but he can't figure Victoria Bennett out—maybe because his longing for the beautiful midwife is so unexpected! He'd come home to the mountains seeking refuge from a world that demanded more than he could give; why now did he have to meet a woman who awakened his need to touch and be touched? Debra weaves a moving story of trust and healing that you won't forget.

Donna Kauffman invites you to meet a **BOUNTY HUNTER,** LOVESWEPT # 707. Kane Hawthorne was hired to locate a runaway wife, but when he finds Elizabeth Lawson, he knows he has to claim her as his own! A desperate woman who dares trust no one, she tries to keep him from making her enemies his, but Kane insists on fighting her demons. And she has no choice but to cherish her savage hero until his own ghosts are silenced. With this electrifying romance Donna proves that nobody does it better when it comes to writing about a dangerous and sexy man.

Cindy Gerard's newest book will keep you awake long **INTO THE NIGHT,** LOVESWEPT # 708. It began as a clever gimmick to promote a radio show for lovers, but the spirited sparring between Jessie Fox and Tony Falcone is so believable, listeners demand to know more of their steamy romance! Jessie vows it is impossible for this gorgeous younger man to want her with the fire she sees burning in his eyes —until the brash Falcon sets a seductive trap his Fox can't escape. Cindy's irresistible blend of humor and playful passion creates a memorable couple you will cherish.

The ever popular Peggy Webb has written her most sensual and heartbreaking novel yet with **ONLY HIS TOUCH,** LOVESWEPT # 709. For years Kathleen Shaw's body had danced to the music of Hunter La Farge's mouth and hands, but when the beautiful ballerina loses everything she'd lived for in a shocking accident, the untamed adventurer is the last man she wants to face. Twice before he'd lost the woman who shared his soul, but now the fierce panther who had claimed her for all time must set her free to recapture her dream. This is Peggy at her best —keep a box of tissues handy!

I'd like to take this opportunity to share with you some exciting news. I have been promoted to Deputy Publisher here at Bantam and will consequently be managing all aspects of the Bantam adult hardcover, trade, and mass-market paperback publishing program. I will continue to oversee women's fiction, but most of the hands-on work will be handled by Senior Editor Beth de Guzman, Assistant Editor Shauna Summers, and Administrative Editor Gina Iemolo. Of course, none of this changes our team's continuing goal to bring you the best in contemporary romantic fiction written by the most talented and loved authors in the genre.

Happy reading!

With warmest wishes,

Nita Taublib

Nita Taublib
Deputy Publisher

P.S. Don't miss the exciting women's novels from Bantam that are coming your way in September— **ADAM'S FALL** is the paperback reprint of the classic romantic novel from *New York Times* bestselling author Sandra Brown; **THE LAST BACHELOR,** from nationally bestselling author Betina Krahn, is a spectacularly entertaining battle of the sexes set in Victorian England; **PRINCE OF WOLVES,** by Susan Krinard, is a spellbinding new romance of mystery, magic, and forbidden passion in the tradition of Linda Lael Miller; and **WHISPERED LIES** is the latest novel from Christy Cohen, about two intimate strangers divided by dangerous secrets, broken vows, and misplaced passions. We'll be giving you a sneak peek at these terrific books in next month's LOVE-SWEPTs. And immediately following this page look for a preview of the exciting romances from Bantam that are *available now!*

Don't miss these electrifying books by your favorite Bantam authors

On sale in July:

MIDNIGHT WARRIOR
by Iris Johansen

BLUE MOON
by Luanne Rice

VELVET
by Jane Feather

WITCH DANCE
by Peggy Webb

Iris Johansen

THE *NEW YORK TIMES* BESTSELLING
AUTHOR OF
THE BELOVED SCOUNDREL

MIDNIGHT WARRIOR

From the author who has been lauded as "the Mistress of Romantic Fantasy" comes a passionate new tale of danger, adventure, and romance that sweeps from a Saxon stronghold to a lovers' bower in the cool, jade-green forests of Wales. . . .

Brynn hesitated for a moment and then said reluctantly, "This is a bad place. Can't you feel it?"

"Feel what?"

"If you cannot feel it, I can't explain. I just want to be gone from here." She paused and then whispered, "Please."

He looked at her in surprise. "This must mean a good deal to you. You're more given to commands than pleas."

She didn't answer.

"What if I give you what you wish?" He lowered his voice to silky softness. "Will you give me a gift in turn?"

"I've given you a gift. Your friend Malik is alive. Isn't that enough for you?"

"It should be."

"But it isn't?"

"Malik will tell you I don't know the meaning of enough. The prize just over the horizon is always the sweetest."

"So you reach out and take it," she said flatly.

"Or barter for it. I prefer the latter. It suits my merchant's soul. I suppose Malik has told you that I'm more trader than knight?"

"No, he said you were the son of a king and capable of being anything you wanted to be."

"Which obviously did not impress you."

"Why should it? It does not matter their station, men are all the same."

He smiled. "Certainly in some aspects. You didn't answer. Will you barter with me?"

"I have nothing with which to barter."

"You're a woman. A woman always has great bartering power."

She straightened her shoulders and turned to look directly at him. "You mean you wish me to be your whore."

His lips tightened. "Your words lack a certain delicacy."

"They do not lack truth." She looked down into the pot. "You wish me to part my limbs and let you rut like a beast of the forest. I wonder you even seek to bargain. You think me your slave. Isn't a slave to be used?"

"Yes," he said curtly. "A slave is to work and give

pleasure. And you're right, I don't have to bargain with you. I can do what I wish."

"I'm glad that is clear." She stirred faster, harder. "Shall we go into the tent now? Or perhaps you wish to take me in front of all your soldiers? I'd be grateful if you'd have the kindness to let me finish preparing this salve that is making your friend well and healthy. But if I seem unreasonable, you must only tell me and I will—"

"Be silent!" His teeth clenched, he added, "I've never met a woman with such a—"

"I'm only being humble and obliging. Isn't that what you want of me?"

"I want—" He stopped and then said thickly, "I'm not certain what I want . . . yet. When I do, I'll be sure you're made fully aware of it."

"Rice has an elegant style, a sharp eye
and a real warmth. In her hands
families—and their values—seem worth
cherishing."
—*San Francisco Chronicle*

BLUE MOON

BY

Luanne Rice

BLUE MOON is a moving novel of a family that discovers the everyday magic of life and the extraordinary power of love. The New York Times *has already praised it as "a rare combination of realism and romance."* Entertainment Weekly *has simply called it "brilliant," and* People *has raved that it is "eloquent . . . a moving and complete tale of the complicated phenomenon we call family."*

Here is a look at this powerful novel. . . .

After two weeks at sea, Billy Medieros was heading home. He usually loved this part of the trip, when the hold was full of fish and his crew was happy because they knew their share of the catch would be high, and they'd all sleep in their own beds that night. He drove the *Norboca*—the best boat in his father-in-law's fleet —around Minturn Ledge, and Mount Hope came into view.

Billy stood at the wheel. The tide had been against

him, and he knew he had missed Cass. She would have left work by now, was probably already home cooking supper. He could picture her at the stove, stirring something steamy, her summer dress sticking damply to her breasts and hips. His wife had the body of a young sexpot. Other guys at sea would pray to Miss July, but Billy would look at pictures of Cass, her coppery curls falling across her face, her blue eyes sexy and mysterious, delicate fingers cupping her full breasts, offering them to the camera. She had given him a Minolta for his last birthday, but for his real present she had posed nude.

Lately, to Billy, Cass had seemed more real in his bunk at sea than she was at home. In person, Cass looked the same, she smelled the same, but she seemed absent, somehow. Raising Josie changed her every day, and Billy resisted the transformation. He missed his wife.

He was nearly home. His eyes roved the church spires, the wooden piers clawing the harbor, American flags flapping from the yacht club and every hotel roof, white yachts rocking on the waves, two trawlers heading out. He waved to the skippers, both of whom he had fished with before. Manuel Vega waved back, a beer in his hand.

Billy couldn't stand skippers who drank onboard. It set a bad example for the crew. You had to stay keen every second. Billy had seen terrible things happen to fishermen who weren't paying attention—fingers lost to a winch handle, a skull split open by a boom. On Billy's first trip out with his father-in-law, Jimmy Keating, a crewmate with both hands busy setting nets had bitten down on a skinny line to hold it in place, and a gust of wind had yanked out six of his top teeth.

Stupid. Billy had no patience for stupid crew

members, and dulling your senses with alcohol, at sea on a fifty-foot boat, was stupid.

"Docking!" Billy yelled, and four guys ran up from below. John Barnard, Billy's first mate for this trip, stood with Billy at the bridge. They had gone to high school together; they'd fished as a team hundreds of times. They never confided in each other, but they had an easygoing way of passing time for long stretches.

Strange, maybe, considering that John Barnard was the only man Billy had ever felt jealous of. Cass liked him too much.

Not that anything had ever happened. But Billy knew she'd get that look in her eyes whenever she was going to see John. Before Christmas parties, Holy Ghost Society Dances, even goddamn PTA meetings. Cass was a flirt, for sure; it only made Billy that much prouder she belonged to him.

Cass and John had dated a couple of times after high school, when Cass had wanted to marry Billy and Billy had been too dumb to ask. Billy, delivering scallops to Lobsterville one night, had met Cass's mother in the kitchen.

"I want to show you something," Mary Keating said. She began leading Billy into the dining room.

"I can't go in there," Billy said, sniffing his sleeve. His rubber boots tracked fragments of scallop shells.

"You'd better, if you don't want to lose her," Mary said. Five-two in her red high heels, Mary Keating had a husky smoker's voice and the drive of a Detroit diesel. Standing in the kitchen doorway, blocking waiters, she pointed across the dining room. There, at a table for two, framed by a picture window overlooking a red sun setting over Mount Hope harbor, were Cass and John having dinner together.

Bonnie and Nora, in their waitress uniforms, hovered nearby.

John was tall, with sandy-brown hair and a movie-hero profile, and the way he and Cass were leaning across the table, smiling into each other's eyes, made Billy want to vault across the bar and smash John's face into his plate. He left without a word, but the incident brought Billy to his senses; two months later, he and Cass were married.

Billy pulled back on the throttle as they passed the No Wake buoy.

"Almost there," John said.

"Can I grab a ride with you?" Billy asked. The Barnards, like most fishing families, lived in Alewives Park.

"Sure," John said. "No problem."

The deck hands checked the dock lines, then stood along the port rail, waiting to jump ashore. Billy threw the engine into reverse, then eased the boat ahead. She bumped hard once, hard again, and then settled into a gentle sway.

In the bestselling tradition of
Amanda Quick, a spectacular new
historical romance from the nationally
bestselling

Jane Feather

"An author to treasure."
—*Romantic Times*

VELVET

*Clad in black velvet and posing as a widowed French com-
tesse, Gabrielle de Beaucaire had returned to England for
one purpose only—to ruin the man responsible for her
young lover's death. But convincing the forbidding Nathaniel Praed, England's greatest spymaster, that she
would make the perfect agent for his secret service would
not be easy. And even after Gabrielle had lured the devastatingly attractive lord to her bed, she would have to con-
tend with his distrust—and with the unexpected hunger
that his merest touch aroused. . . .*

It was a bright clear night, the air crisp, the stars
sharp in the limitless black sky. He flung open the
window, leaning his elbows on the sill, looking out
over the expanse of smooth lawn where frost glittered

under the starlight. It would be a beautiful morning for the hunt.

He climbed back into bed and blew out his candle.

He heard the rustling of the woodbine almost immediately. His hand slipped beneath his pillow to his constant companion, the small silver-mounted pistol. He lay very still, every muscle held in waiting, his ears straining into the darkness. The small scratching, rustling sounds continued, drawing closer to the open window. Someone was climbing the thick ancient creeper clinging to the mellow brick walls of the Jacobean manor house.

His hand closed more firmly over the pistol and he hitched himself up on one elbow, his eyes on the square of the window, waiting.

Hands competently gripped the edge of the windowsill, followed by a dark head. The nocturnal visitor swung a leg over the sill and hitched himself upright, straddling the sill.

"Since you've only just snuffed your candle, I'm sure you're still awake," Gabrielle de Beaucaire said into the dark, still room. "And I'm sure you have a pistol, so please don't shoot, it's only me."

Nathaniel was rarely taken by surprise and was a master at concealing it on those rare occasions. On this occasion, however, his training deserted him.

"*Only!*" he exclaimed. "What the hell are you doing?"

"Guess," his visitor challenged cheerfully from her perch.

"You'll have to forgive me, but I don't find guessing games amusing," he declared in clipped accents. He sat up, his pistol still in his hand, and stared at the dark shape outlined against the moonlight. That aura of trouble surrounding Gabrielle de Beaucaire had not been a figment of his imagination.

"Perhaps I should be flattered," he said icily. "Am I to assume unbridled lust lies behind the honor of this visit, madam?" His eyes narrowed.

Disconcertingly, the woman appeared to be impervious to irony. She laughed. A warm, merry sound that Nathaniel found as incongruous in the circumstances as it was disturbingly attractive.

"Not at his point, Lord Praed; but there's no saying what the future might hold." It was a mischievous and outrageous statement that rendered him temporarily speechless.

She took something out of the pocket of her britches and held it on the palm of her hand. "I'm here to present my credentials."

She swung off the windowsill and approached the bed, a sinuous figure in her black britches and glimmering white shirt.

He leaned sideways, struck flint on tinder, and re-lit the bedside candle. The dark red hair glowed in the light as she extended her hand, palm upward, toward him and he saw what she held.

It was a small scrap of black velvet cut with a ragged edge.

"Well, well." The evening's puzzles were finally solved. Lord Praed opened a drawer in the bedside table and took out a piece of tissue paper. Unfolding it, he revealed the twin of the scrap of material.

"I should have guessed," he said pensively. "Only a woman would have come up with such a fanciful idea." He took the velvet from her extended palm and fitted the ragged edge to the other piece, making a whole square. "So you're Simon's surprise. No wonder he was so secretive. But what makes you think I would ever employ a woman?"

WITCH DANCE

BY

Peggy Webb

"Ms. Webb has an inventive mind brimming with
originality that makes all of her books special
reading."—*Romantic Times*

*An exquisite woman of ivory and jade, she'd come to
Witch Dance, Oklahoma, to bring modern medicine to the
native Chickasaw people. But when Dr. Kate Malone saw
the magnificent Indian rising from the river, naked as sin
and twice as tempting, every thought of duty was lost,
drowned in a primitive wave of longing that made her
tremble with desire. . . .*

He was more man than she'd ever seen. And every
gorgeous inch of him was within touching distance.

For all he seemed to care, he could have been
bending over her in a Brooks Brothers suit.

"What impulse sent you into the river?" He
squatted beside her with both hands on her shoulders, and she'd never felt skin as hot in her life.

" I thought you were drowning."

His laughter was deep and melodious, and as sensual as exotic music played in some dark corner of a
dimly lit café where lovers embraced.

"I am Chickasaw," he said, as if that explained
everything.

"Well, I'm human and I made a mistake." She
pushed her wet hair away from her face. "Why can't

you just admit you made a mistake, staying under the water so long I thought you were going to drown?"

"You were watching me?"

"No . . . yes . . ." His legs were powerful, heavily muscled, bent in such a way that the best parts of him were hidden. He leaned closer, intent on answers. How did he expect her to think straight with his leg touching hers like that? "Not deliberately," she said. "I was on a picnic. How did I know you'd be cavorting about in the river without any clothes on?"

He searched her face with eyes deep and black. Then he touched her cheeks, his strong hands exquisitely gentle.

"I'm sorry I ruined your picnic." Ever so tenderly his hands roamed over her face. Breathless, she sat beside the river, his willing captive. "You've scratched your face . . . here . . . and here."

Until that moment she hadn't known that every nerve in the body could tremble. Now she could attest to it as a medical fact.

". . . and your legs." He gave her legs the same tender attention he'd given her face. She would have sold her soul to feel his hands on her forever. "I have remedies for your injuries."

Oh, God. Would he kiss them and make them well? She almost said it.

"I can fix them . . ." How? She could barely breathe. "I'm a doctor."

"You came to Tribal Lands to practice medicine?"

"You doubt my word?"

"No. Your commitment."

"Is it because I'm white that you think I'm not committed, or because I'm female?"

"Neither, *Wictonaye*." In one fluid movement he stood before her, smiling.

And in that moment her world changed. Colors

and light receded, faded, until there was nothing except the bold Chickasaw with his glowing, polished skin and his seductive voice that obliterated every thought, every need except the most basic . . . to die of love. Sitting on the hard ground, looking up at her nameless captor, she wanted to die in the throes of passion.

She stood on shaky, uncertain legs. Clenching her fists by her side, she faced him.

"If you're going to call me names, use English, please."

"*Wictonaye* . . . wildcat."

"I've been called worse." Would God forgive her if she left right now? Would He give her the healing touch and allow her to save lives if she forgot about her lust and focused on her mission?

She spun around, then felt his hand on her arm.

"I've been rude. It's not my way."

"Nor mine." She grinned. "Except sometimes."

"You tried to save my life, and I don't know your name."

"Kate Malone."

"Thank you for saving my life, Kate Malone." His eyes sparkled with wicked glee. She'd never known a man of such boldness . . . nor such appeal. "I'm Eagle Mingo."

"Next time you decide to play in the river, Eagle Mingo, be more careful. I might not be around to rescue you."

She marched toward the bluff, thinking it was a good exit, until he appeared beside her, still naked as sin and twice as tempting.

"You forgot your shoe." He held out one of her moccasins.

"Thanks." Lord, did he expect her to bend down

and put it on with him standing there like that? She hobbled along, half shoeless.

"And your picnic basket." He scooped it off the ground and handed it to her. Then, damned if he didn't bow like some courtly knight in shining armor.

If she ever got home, she'd have to take an aspirin and go to bed. Doctor's orders.

"Good-bye. Enjoy your"—her eyes raked him from head to toe, and she could feel her whole body getting hot—"swim."

She didn't know how she got up the bluff, but she didn't draw a good breath until she was safely at the top. He was still standing down there, looking up. She could feel his eyes on her.

Lest he think she was a total coward, she put on her other shoe, then turned and casually waved at him. At least she hoped it was casual.

Dammit all, he waved back. Facing full front. She might never recover.

And don't miss these incredible romances from Bantam Books, on sale in August:

THE LAST BACHELOR

by the nationally bestselling author

Betina Krahn

"One of the genre's most creative writers."
—*Romantic Times*

PRINCE OF WOLVES

by the sensational

Susan Krinard

A romance of mystery, magic, and forbidden passion

WHISPERED LIES

by the highly acclaimed

Christy Cohen

A novel of dangerous desires and seductive secrets

OFFICIAL RULES

To enter the sweepstakes below carefully follow all instructions found elsewhere in this offer.

The **Winners Classic** will award prizes with the following approximate maximum values: 1 Grand Prize: $26,500 (or $25,000 cash alternate); 1 First Prize: $3,000; 5 Second Prizes: $400 each; 35 Third Prizes: $100 each; 1,000 Fourth Prizes: $7.50 each. Total maximum retail value of Winners Classic Sweepstakes is $42,500. Some presentations of this sweepstakes may contain individual entry numbers corresponding to one or more of the aforementioned prize levels. To determine the Winners, individual entry numbers will first be compared with the winning numbers preselected by computer. For winning numbers not returned, prizes will be awarded in random drawings from among all eligible entries received. Prize choices may be offered at various levels. If a winner chooses an automobile prize, all license and registration fees, taxes, destination charges and, other expenses not offered herein are the responsibility of the winner. If a winner chooses a trip, travel must be complete within one year from the time the prize is awarded. Minors must be accompanied by an adult. Travel companion(s) must also sign release of liability. Trips are subject to space and departure availability. Certain black-out dates may apply.

The following applies to the sweepstakes named above:

No purchase necessary. You can also enter the sweepstakes by sending your name and address to: P.O. Box 508, Gibbstown, N.J. 08027. Mail each entry separately. Sweepstakes begins 6/1/93. Entries must be received by 12/30/94. Not responsible for lost, late, damaged, misdirected, illegible or postage due mail. Mechanically reproduced entries are not eligible. All entries become property of the sponsor and will not be returned.

Prize Selection/Validations: Selection of winners will be conducted no later than 5:00 PM on January 28, 1995, by an independent judging organization whose decisions are final. Random drawings will be held at 1211 Avenue of the Americas, New York, N.Y. 10036. Entrants need not be present to win. Odds of winning are determined by total number of entries received. Circulation of this sweepstakes is estimated not to exceed 200 million. All prizes are guaranteed to be awarded and delivered to winners. Winners will be notified by mail and may be required to complete an affidavit of eligibility and release of liability which must be returned within 14 days of date on notification or alternate winners will be selected in a random drawing. Any prize notification letter or any prize returned to a participating sponsor, Bantam Doubleday Dell Publishing Group, Inc., its participating divisions or subsidiaries, or the independent judging organization as undeliverable will be awarded to an alternate winner. Prizes are not transferable. No substitution for prizes except as offered or as may be necessary due to unavailability, in which case a prize of equal or greater value will be awarded. Prizes will be awarded approximately 90 days after the drawing. All taxes are the sole responsibility of the winners. Entry constitutes permission (except where prohibited by law) to use winners' names, hometowns, and likenesses for publicity purposes without further or other compensation. Prizes won by minors will be awarded in the name of parent or legal guardian.

Participation: Sweepstakes open to residents of the United States and Canada, except for the province of Quebec. Sweepstakes sponsored by Bantam Doubleday Dell Publishing Group, Inc., (BDD), 1540 Broadway, New York, NY 10036. Versions of this sweepstakes with different graphics and prize choices will be offered in conjunction with various solicitations or promotions by different subsidiaries and divisions of BDD. Where applicable, winners will have their choice of any prize offered at level won. Employees of BDD, its divisions, subsidiaries, advertising agencies, independent judging organization, and their immediate family members are not eligible.

Canadian residents, in order to win, must first correctly answer a time limited arithmetical skill testing question. Void in Puerto Rico, Quebec and wherever prohibited or restricted by law. Subject to all federal, state, local and provincial laws and regulations. For a list of major prize winners (available after 1/29/95): send a self-addressed, stamped envelope entirely separate from your entry to: Sweepstakes Winners, P.O. Box 517, Gibbstown, NJ 08027. Requests must be received by 12/30/94. DO NOT SEND ANY OTHER CORRESPONDENCE TO THIS P.O. BOX.

SWP 7/93

Bestselling Women's Fiction

Sandra Brown

_____	28951-9	TEXAS! LUCKY	$5.99/6.99 in Canada
_____	28990-X	TEXAS! CHASE	$5.99/6.99
_____	29500-4	TEXAS! SAGE	$5.99/6.99
_____	29085-1	22 INDIGO PLACE	$5.99/6.99
_____	29783-X	A WHOLE NEW LIGHT	$5.99/6.99
_____	56045-X	TEMPERATURES RISING	$5.99/6.99
_____	56274-6	FANTA C	$4.99/5.99
_____	56278-9	LONG TIME COMING	$4.99/5.99

Amanda Quick

_____	28354-5	SEDUCTION	$5.99/6.99
_____	28932-2	SCANDAL	$5.99/6.99
_____	28594-7	SURRENDER	$5.99/6.99
_____	29325-7	RENDEZVOUS	$5.99/6.99
_____	29316-8	RECKLESS	$5.99/6.99
_____	29316-8	RAVISHED	$4.99/5.99
_____	29317-6	DANGEROUS	$5.99/6.99
_____	56506-0	DECEPTION	$5.99/7.50

Nora Roberts

_____	29078-9	GENUINE LIES	$5.99/6.99
_____	28578-5	PUBLIC SECRETS	$5.99/6.99
_____	26461-3	HOT ICE	$5.99/6.99
_____	26574-1	SACRED SINS	$5.99/6.99
_____	27859-2	SWEET REVENGE	$5.99/6.99
_____	27283-7	BRAZEN VIRTUE	$5.99/6.99
_____	29597-7	CARNAL INNOCENCE	$5.50/6.50
_____	29490-3	DIVINE EVIL	$5.99/6.99

Iris Johansen

_____	29871-2	LAST BRIDGE HOME	$4.50/5.50
_____	29604-3	THE GOLDEN BARBARIAN	$4.99/5.99
_____	29244-7	REAP THE WIND	$4.99/5.99
_____	29032-0	STORM WINDS	$4.99/5.99
_____	28855-5	THE WIND DANCER	$4.95/5.95
_____	29968-9	THE TIGER PRINCE	$5.50/6.50
_____	29944-1	THE MAGNIFICENT ROGUE	$5.99/6.99
_____	29945-X	BELOVED SCOUNDREL	$5.99/6.99

Ask for these titles at your bookstore or use this page to order.

Please send me the books I have checked above. I am enclosing $ _____ (add $2.50 to cover postage and handling). Send check or money order, no cash or C. O. D.'s please.

Mr./ Ms. _____

Address _____

City/ State/ Zip _____

Send order to: Bantam Books, Dept. FN 16, 2451 S. Wolf Road, Des Plaines, IL 60018

Please allow four to six weeks for delivery.

Prices and availability subject to change without notice.   FN 16 - 4/94